CUB BOY TRAINING

First Edition

Published by The Nazca Plains Corporation
Las Vegas, Nevada
2010

ISBN: 978-1-935509-81-3

Published by

The Nazca Plains Corporation ®
4640 Paradise Rd, Suite 141
Las Vegas NV 89109-8000

PUBLISHER'S NOTE
Cub Boy Training is a work of fiction created wholly by *Bret Yerlac*'s
imagination. All characters are fictional and any resemblance to any
persons living or deceased is purely by accident. No portion of this
book reflects any real person or events.

Male Cover Photos
Denis Tevekov and Borko Ćirić

Art Director
Blake Stephens

CUB BOY TRAINING

First Edition

Bret Yerlac

CHAPTER 1

I was born and raised in a very small town east of San Francisco in the central California foothills of the Sierra-Nevada Mountains; however my dad grew up in San Francisco. In fact, my paternal grandmother still lived in the same house on Scott Street in the Marina District where my dad and his two brothers were raised. Every summer since I can remember, I spent most of my summer vacations from school with Grandma and Grandpa in the beautiful 'City by the Bay.' After Grandpa died, I spent every summer with Grandma. She liked the company and the family liked someone living with her now that she was pushing 80. I loved her and the city life was for me, especially the Marina, with its salt air and noted for being one of the warmer areas to live in the city where cold fog rolls in almost every night during the summers making it downright cold until it burns off mid morning the next day. Right after I turned 18, one mid morning summer day, I was kicking around the Marina District as usual watching the many yachts come and go from their births along the long piers where they were moored on my own in just a pair of tennis shoes, sweat socks, a big sloppy 49er's sweatshirt, a pair of baggy low rider denims, and of course, my pride and joy, the SF49er's football team cap I inherited from dear Gramps. Damn how he loved that team and would take me regularly to most the home games, back then at Keiser Stadium located on the southeast corner of Golden Gate Park.

There was a single guy jogging about this time every morning that always slowed, smiled and said hello son as he passed. Sure enough, here he came along again. I could have set my clock to his appearance each morning, only this time he stopped, smiled, and made conversation. He was tall, masculine, very good-looking, very lean and muscular, probably in his late 30's to mid 40's. He asked me if I was waiting for anyone in particular. When I told him no, just watching the yacht club's usual activity this time of morning, he asked me if I wanted to jog with him for awhile. I figured, why not, and off we went, him talking up a storm, me listening mostly. He did ask me a few questions as we jogged side by side for awhile - my age, and my name. I just gave him my first name, Joey. Eventually he asked where I lived, and finally, where I was staying in S.F. to be out and about every morning so early. When I told him I spent every summer with my Grandma, he asked a few questions about her - her age, and her health, where her home was located. He asked if I was going on to college. I told him I received an acceptance letter from S.F. State and would be starting the fall semester after summer vacation and living with Grandma. He seemed legitimately interested in carrying on a regular conversation with me. After about half an hour of some very aggressive jogging, we circled back to the block between Lyon and Baker Streets on Marina Blvd. and he stopped. We both stood, beaded with perspiration; the sweat was dripping off our faces as he pointed up to the house we were facing. All the houses along Marina Blvd. are crammed together on narrow but deep lots and most are two and three story beauties with garages on the first ground floor. The house we faced, like all the others along the Blvd. facing the water, was exceptionally beautiful. Like all the other homes facing the ocean along Marina Blvd., it was an absolute showplace.

"I live here son; it looks like you could use a cold drink too, exceptionally warm this morning for the city, usually it is much cooler and windy. We are certainly overdressed for this weather today. Come on up and I'll fix us right up with a cold drink." He seemed safe enough, so I following him along the narrow side yard, through an electronically locked gate leading into a formal garden and patio area, up a short flight of stairs and right in through the back entrance to his house. We ended up in the kitchen where he produced a couple of beers from the refrigerator. "Sorry Joey, I'm out of sodas, only have beer, but what the hell, that's OK! One will not kill you - Heineken, the good stuff! Have a seat and relax and we will cool down." He took off his sweat soaked sweatshirt and threw it on the table. It damn near landed in my lap had my arm not stopped it where it rested on the tabletop. His strong masculine aroma rose from that sweatshirt and his strong male scent and pheromones filled the air! My libido immediately awakened and my defenses lowered inhaling his strong male scent. Woof! What a rush! As I inhaled his scent I looked him over, trying to be coy about it. He obviously sensed my interest in his finely tuned body, especially when I realized he was looking through the glass top kitchen table at the tent that was forming in my old worn baggies that had shrunk and fit far tighter than normal in the crotch, and here I was going commando this morning without the support of a jock or undershorts. By that time it dawned on me that he had a full view, it was useless to try and hide my fully expanded boner from his eyes. I just let my hormones go rampant and ignored my hard-on and let it expand and pulsate, forming a wet spot on the tented material. Between inhaling his strong masculine scent and watching his sweaty muscled upper torso flex with his every movement, I was mesmerized and unable to quit overtly staring at his magnificence.

He was very tan, rippled with muscles and had a marine emblem tattooed on one arm, a big black leopard that covered the full length of his other arm, from his upper arm and down his forearm nearly to his wrist. Huge big tuffs of black hair protruded from under each armpit, and a string of long black hair started between his pictorials, tapered down to about an inch wide and continued right down the middle of his torso, over his abs, circled his navel and ran down the center of his torso and disappeared below his waistband. It was an awesome sight, as my dad and the men in my family have very little body hair. What we do have is so light blond it is barely noticeable. I couldn't keep from staring, as hard as I tried. He was just too handsomely awesome, so I just relaxed back in the chair, spread my feet out wide, and enjoyed letting my full boner pulsate and leak cock-snot into my faded light colored baggies. I was overheated, sweating, nervous and obviously turned on to this guy just watching him pace back and forth flexing muscles and constantly adjusting his own expanding bulge, until it expand, lengthened and snaked up hard against his waistband. Like a turtle's head, the head was soon poking its way into view exposing a cockhead half covered with a liberal foreskin and begin to bubble cock-snot. I watched it dribble and caught myself softly moaning unconsciously. My heart was thumping watching this peep show he was orchestrating.

"Mmmm! Mmmm! Nice tattoos and muscles mister," I blurted out thinking it would cover up what I was really gawking at now so openly. I found myself blushing deep red I'm sure, embarrassed after letting that slip from my loose tongue, again without even thinking what I was saying. I wondered if the beer, which I had never really had a taste for, had loosened my tongue and relaxed me enough to come out with my observations of his body so verbally.

A big smile flashed across his face as he responded with, "Well thanks! I do try to take care of myself and always look my best." He went into a few Charles Atlas muscle poses, still bringing no special attention to his exposed drooling cockhead. He made his pictorials alternately jump and it was then I really noticed how large his nipples had grown. They could only be described as huge, stiff and sexy. Before he stopped he made his wash board abs roll like waves coming in off the ocean floor. Each roll or his abs seemed to lift and expand and make his boner pulsate and spew more juice. This guy was obviously seriously into bodybuilding. His entire body was awesome, glistening with sweat and a perfect example and testament to just how a middle aged guy can keep himself tuned and in excellent physical shape and have total control over muscles, including his boner. Oh my, my!

I always liked the smell of my dad when I would crawl into bed with him and mom when I was much younger. Never really knew why, but his smell always was very welcome to my senses. However, the pheromones coming off this guy were almost visible with the naked eye they were so pungent and intoxicating. My obvious boner continued to throb and leak as I soaked up the physical masculinity of the guy. I unconsciously picked up his sweatshirt and put it to my nose and inhaled the powerful aroma as I continued to stare at the guy who obviously knew the affect he was having on my libido before I realized what I was doing and sat it back down quickly, only to pick it right back up and put it back to my nose. He let out a little chuckle, adjusted his equipment, pulling the waistband down a bit more so he could work the foreskin completely down exposing his huge mushroom shaped glands. He gave it a couple of strokes and lifted a good supply of cock-snot with his index finger and put it to his tongue, smiled and squeezed another ample amount on to his finger, leaned over the table and rubbed it on my lips. My tongue immediately responded by licking my lips. I smiled at him as he loaded up the finger again and this time stuck it right between my waiting open lips. He smiled again but said absolutely nothing about what he had done. It seemed like an eternity before he spoke again. He then continued addressing my interest in his tattoos and muscles.

"Yea, got the tats in Vietnam, spent two hitches in that hell hole. I work out a lot to keep in shape, jog every morning now that I am retired. It's important at my age." I sat there in his kitchen watching him as he continued to pace back and forth, talking to me non stop in a monotone voice. I no sooner finished the beer and he had another open and sitting in front of me. "Drink up son, one more to loosen you up a bit. We both worked up quite a sweat, got the good old male juices flowing out of more places than just our pores. Good smell, a man after he exercises and works up a good sweat! Makes the old pecker want to stand up and dance the jig too." He was on his third Heineken, still pacing around the kitchen walking and talking up a storm in that monotone voice. He watched my eyes follow him, constantly cupping and scratching his balls and crotch and tweaking his nipples. I could clearly see his dick was really drooling now. My eyes were glued to every movement of his muscled body. Yea, I was staring alright. He just kept circling around like a lion stalking its' prey, sucking on his beer, rubbing his stomach, and constantly readjusting his equipment. He obviously was wearing an old jock that was stretched enough at the waist to allow his cock to push through like it had, but it had to be getting uncomfortable on his balls. I could no longer keep my eyes from following his every move and my mind from tuning in on his monotone voice as his conversation switched to sex and dirty talk. The strong male scent coming off him, mixing with my own scent and filling the room and watching his antics and muscles flex, my pecker was stirring big time in my baggies and tenting in my boxers. A big old wet spot had formed making the mushroomed glands around my cockhead totally visible through the thin white material of my tight shorts.

I was getting very turned on watching him. That second Heineken had me very relaxed. My eyes continued to follow him, and I felt a persistent warm surge spread in my groin demanding immediate attention. Without even realizing what I was doing, my hand covered my crotch and I boldly begin to squeeze and fondle myself. I think his monotone voice talking non stop about all the sex on internet sites, his smile, white teeth flashing and muscles flexing had me mesmerized, maybe even hypnotized. When he started talking about guys fucking around on the internet, he obviously noticed my state as he approached me and swung my chair away from the table and observed me straight on for a moment, eye to eye!

"Hey kid, what say we get that heavy sweatshirt off you and get you cooled off a bit, make you more comfortable; you must be burning up in there after that second beer. You're sweating like a stuck hog!" He lifted my arms over my head and had my sweatshirt up and off me in one quick movement. It was all done before I could even come back to reality or focus my eyes on him again. "There, that's better; you will feel better now! Let that young body breath.

He rubbed his hands through my blond hair, then up and down over my bare chest a couple of times pinching my nipples each time. He mumbled, "I see someone likes nipple play, and what's this we have going on down here?" He grabbed me by the crotch and had his hand round my dick in a split second stroking my full boner. He chuckled to himself again, then grabbed me around the waist and lifted me on to my feet, spun me around with his crotch against my buns. He repositioned his one arm around my neck holding my back arched so his boner stayed firmly pressed and throbbing in place. The other hand never let go of my dick. I finally came out of my stupor enough to put up some physical resistance, but I was no match for his strength. He continued to rub his boner back and forth and up and down over my buns as he slowly jacked me until I was panting and just about ready to shoot in my sweats. I had never had a guy make me feel this great before, when he stopped abruptly and let go of my dick and rubbed his hand and fingers up and down over my bare torso stopping at my nipple and worked it over severely between his powerful fingers.

"Oh yea, I see you like my big dick rubbing your bottom and my fingers working your sweet nips. Well there is more to experience that you are sure to enjoy even more my little Cub-Boy."

He held me, his huge boner pressed tightly over the crack of my ass and bitch walked me, protesting, and somewhat fighting him for release down a hallway to a room he had all set up as a weight/ play room. I think I was more excited than scared at the moment, as I was so turned on to the guy being so masculine and dominant with me. He immediately stripped me of all my clothing, stuffed one of my socks into my mouth, and put a leather belt apparatus around my thighs that secured my wrists in Velcro firmly to my sides.

"Now settle down boy, I don't want to have to hurt you, but I will if you don't calm down and learn to take orders like a good Marine Grunt." I still was giving him a little struggle. He gave me a quick swift punch in the gut and I folded. He then sat on a padded bench and pulled me face down over his knees. He proceeded to paddle my ass and after 10 strong smacks with the palm of his hand on my bare bottom, he stopped the assault. My ass was burning and had to be bright red from the heat I was feeling from the whipping.

He lifted me up on to my feet and I realized I was still sporting a full-fledged hard-on that had been leaking cock-snot between his inner thighs. He smiled as he watched my cock pulsate and continue to leak and bounce as I rose to my feet with his help. "I think you liked that little attitude adjusting exercise, just look at that boner you're sporting son." I looked down and realized he was right, but just ignored his remark. At 18, I had been jacking off regularly, but I was still almost a 100 percent virgin, never been with another person, except with my dad when I was too young to even cal it sex. I especially never had been with another guy before like this. When he buried his face in my crotch and started sucking my cock into his mouth, I got all excited and I just fell into this sexual pleasure in a big way naturally. He only sucked on me long enough to get me really liking his assault; my cock was hard and oozing pre-cum. Then he stopped sucking abruptly, looked up and made eye contact smiling.

"You like that son; I can tell! Obviously your first time getting your cock sucked I bet! Well, wait until you feel the good stuff I'm going to teach you today. Hold on Baby and don't you dare cum or you're going to feel my wrath again on your ass." He stuck a finger into his mouth and then spread the saliva over and around my little rosebud pucker, circling and massaging. It felt so wonderful that I just relaxed, enjoyed and became more and more submissive. He kept working that magic finger around and over my pucker, constantly keeping me on the edge of shooting my load as he continued to lick the sensitive underside of my cock head. I was moaning and really enjoying the new feelings when all of a sudden he pushed the finger up inside me. Fire broke out in my ass! It was as a hot branding iron had penetrated my shit chute. I rebelled! My muffled screams he ignored, holding me tightly, one finger up my ass, the other arm holding me still. He continued to work that finger up and in me. I finally calmed down and relaxed my ass muscles. As I relaxed, his probing seemed to feel better until the burning sensation turned to a very nice warm feeling inside that seemed to radiate up through my insides. As the warmth spread, I really liked what he was doing inside me with that single finger. It was not long and I realized I had spread my legs out wider and I was assisting, pumping my ass back over his finger, submitting to the new feelings of sheer pleasure going on inside me. He was massaging something that really felt good with that magic finger.

"Looks like you like that too, right kid?" He put two fingers in his mouth this time and inserted them in me. When I was showing signs of pleasure again, he put in the third finger and really spread my ass open. I must admit, it felt absolutely sensational. My cock was dancing against his lips, pre-cum dripping from my cock on to his tongue. He was licking, sniffing and totally lost in his own pleasures. He took one last lick of my cock-snot and abruptly stopped.

"Damn Boy you sure smell and taste great – can't get enough of that sweet 'Nectar of the Gods' you young guys produce! I think you're about ready for the 'Grand Prize' now my little Cub-Boy!" He pulled his running shorts down along with his jock strap the rest of the way and up popped his dick, oozing, pre-cum dripping from the head. He stepped out of both and kicked them aside. He grabbed some lube from the table, greased up his dick, laid me back on the same sturdy table and lifted my legs up and rested them on his shoulders. He slowly pushed his dick up into me, first just the head. He stopped for just long enough for me to relax and catch my breath from the sudden entry. Then he slowly pushed all the way in until I felt his pubic hair against my butt. My cock was dripping and strings of pre-cum were dripping down over my torso.

"Now comes the good stuff little Cub; you're going to love this part!" He slowly started to work his dick in and out of me. He made sure I stayed excited and hard as he worked his slick fingers over my cock head. Each time he took a complete stroke into my ass, it started to feel better and better. He smiled down at me and a warm glow fell upon me. It was beginning to feel terrific and my little 7 inches was oozing and twitching as he rotated on one certain spot inside me that seemed to be a real pleasure zone.

"You like that my little Cub-Boy?" He pulled the sock out of my mouth and asked me again. "You like that don't you? Tell me you like this big dick in you making your little walnut feel so good your cock keeps dripping!" I just moaned as he smiled down at me. He leaned forward and licked, sucked and nipped on my nipples, giving me even more pleasures to consume. My body went into total submission now. I was as a rag doll attached to him. It was remarkable how fast he took possession of my entire being the instant he busted my cherry and worked over my prostrate with the head of his dick. He virtually owned me now and could have done anything he wanted with me and it would have been just plain OK as long as he kept raking, stabbing, and massaging my little walnut size hot button.

"Please release my hands. I will not fight you anymore! I want to be able to touch you too! This feels so good!" He ignored my request. He was dripping with sweat and smelled wonderfully masculine towering over me. I just inhaled his scent as he thrust into me sending warm rushes through my entire body. I was going to shoot if he kept this up much longer. Sure enough, three more hard thrusts and I shot my load all over my chin, chest and stomach. I convulsed with the thrilling feelings that engulfed every cell in my body.

"FUCK, FUCK YES," came from his lips! My ass muscles went wild and he buried his dick in me, stiffened, and I felt his hot sperm unload and fill my ass. He fell forward over me and we both lay helpless as the waves of pleasure flowed through us. I could not help myself from just floating mentally for a while as he covered my lips with his and sucked face for awhile as we returned down to earth.

"You did well for your first time son. You will soon want more and more dick up that tight hot ass poking and massaging your little walnut, bringing you to huge and wonderful anal climaxes. The more dicks you get, the more you are going to crave anal stimulation, the kind that only a real stiff dick on an assertive guy can deliver. You will soon enough understand what I am telling you to be true son."

"Crave Sir? I don't think so, but I must admit it sure is a great feeling alright."

"I've been watching you for about three days now down on the Marina watching the yachts come and go. When I first saw those baby blues and long blond hair, I knew I had to have you as my Cub-Boy. I knew that cute ass of yours was made for fucking the minute I laid eyes on you. You're going to keep your mouth shut about what we did together here today or you are not getting any more anal pleasures from me! Before tomorrow morning arrives, I guarantee you are going to want more of this dick I now have up your ass, up inside you again, stroking and massaging the constant internal throbbing up inside your ass for more anal orgasms like you have experienced for the first time with me today. You hear me good little Cub!" He pulled from me and stood up straight. He pulled me up on to my feet in front of him and scooped up cum that had accumulated on my torso, chin to my crotch. He fed it to me off his fingers, making me lick each clean and dry individually. He then pushed me down on to my knees with my face to his crotch and said, "Now clean me up like a good Cub Boy should for his dominate male. Don't forget the balls too son."

When I had him all cleaned up, he lifted me to my feet in front of him, raised his left arm up and grabbed the back of his neck for support. "Lick my pit nice and dry now son, I'm sure by now you will love the smell and taste of a real man. All Cubs like to lick their Masters pits! Eat my wet, salty pit Boy!" I stepped back, but he grabbed me by the hair again and forced my face to his pit. "Lick and suck the nice musk son; don't let it go to waste. You will love it once you get a good taste and smell for it as all young cub boys soon learn! If you want to be my Cub Trainee boy, you are going to learn to like many things I have planned for you! Now get to work and start sniffing and licking!"

He was indeed wet, hairy and definitely had the taste of salt, the smell of a strong masculine male musk. There was more long hair under his armpit than I had in my groin. The more I licked and sucked, the better it smelled and tasted, until I was really into what I was doing. "See little guy, I told you that you would like it! Now do the other one too!" When I had it nice and clean too, he grabbed my hair again and directed my lips and tongue to his nipple. "Suck on this for awhile too son, I really like my boys to suck and nibble on my nipples." Surrounded with damp musk and hair, they tasted great. "Don't just suck boy, nibble and bite softly on the nipple! That is better! OH YEA! See what you're doing to me again Boy!" I looked down and he was sporting another big hard-on!

"Well, I guess you know what you're going to do for me now don't you?"

Hands on my shoulders, he pressed me down to my knees and slapped the shaft back and forth across my face a few times as cock-snot oozed out over my lips from his pee hole. I finally was able to catch the head between my lips and suck it in. Having tasted it before when I cleaned it and his balls, it was very welcome between my lips. His crotch radiated male pheromones, sending my head again swimming with pleasure. I too had a raging hard-on, which he kept rubbing with his calf and knee, keeping me breathlessly lusting for his dick and balls. I sucked and nibbled on that big beautiful dick. He was not satisfied with me just working on the head and about three inches of the shaft. Soon he had his fingers tightly woven in my golden locks and was forcing me to deep throat him. I was gagging and snot was running from my nostrils, but he did not care. Eventually I felt his entire shaft slip down into my throat and muscles tightened and I stopped gagging. I could not breathe and began to panic until he finally released me enough so I could pull off just far enough to catch my breath. Then in he went again, repeatedly, until I learned to breath and deep throat him properly. With tears in my eyes, and mucus dripping from my nose, he shot a load down my throat, shuddering and moaning in lustful bliss.

When I looked down, I realized I had shot a load on his leg and it was running down over his calf, ankle and heal. He pushed me down. "Clean up your mess boy, you made it, so I assume you like sucking my big dick down your throat too! This is good; next time you will know how I like it!

"YES Sir, just like you like your cock sucked! Would you fuck me again Sir? I really like that more than sucking on your dick!"

"Not today Pussy Boy, but meet me at the Marina tomorrow morning about 7:30am and we can jog again and I'll fuck you again tomorrow morning. Remember well, you say anything to anybody about what we did here today and you will not be getting anymore dick from the MASTER. Now get dressed and get your hot ass out of here until tomorrow. From now on call me SIR or MASTER, and do not wear any underwear tomorrow or jack off tonight! You understand boy?"

"SIR, YES SIR!"

As I was leaving he shouted, "Hey Boy, what's your full name?"

"Joey Schmidt, Sir! See you tomorrow, 7:30am, OK!"

Cub Boy Training – Day 2: Back for more!

It was difficult not jacking off that night after learning to suck cock properly and getting my cherry ass violated. What a fantastic new experience the stranger I met at the Marina gave me yesterday. He got me so turned on to him I spent the most part of the night tossing and turning with a raging hard-on thinking about how great he made me feel when his dick was buried up my Wazoo. I had a dream during the night. He was inside me; his dick was blasting my insides. I awoke suddenly having an organism soaking my P J's. I just rolled over and went right back to sleep feeling satisfied and happy. When I awoke in the morning, my P J's were stuck to me and I had another raging hard-on to try to ignore. Master had given me explicit instructions not to jack-off. I thought, "I still don't know his name or anything about him. All he told me was to call him Sir or Master. What has he done to me to make me so horny for more of what he did to me yesterday?"

By the time Grandma fixed breakfast it was going on to 7:15am. She said I should put on more clothing than my running shorts and a tank top, as the SF fog had rolled in and it was cold outside. She made me change into my sweats before she would let me leave the house for the Marina. By the time I ran the half block or more, it was 7:40am. Master was waiting for me, tapping his foot and looking at his watch. As I approached the stern look on his face said it all.

"Where you been boy? I said to be here at 7:30am... You are damn near 15 minutes late. Harsh discipline is in order later! I do not tolerate tardiness from my Boys! Now get your hot ass over here and let me get a good look at you again." He had a leather-riding crop in his hand and ran it up and down over my body, poking and prodding me, mostly on my ass. "Now get your buns moving boy at a quick trot down that trail there." He was right on my ass prodding me, making me run faster and faster to keep the crop from striking my ass. Though it was damn cold in the morning fog, beads of sweat were forming on my face, neck and body. I was dripping with sweat when he finally shouted, "STOP!"

We were in a thicket of bushes that surrounded the "Legion of Honor" facility next to the duck pond where I had first met him the day before. He pushed me into the bushes, down on my knees and lowered his sweats exposing his flaccid dick and balls. "Now deep throat me Boy, just like I taught you to do yesterday. Get with it or your going to taste some more of this crop on a bare ass!" I guess I hesitated just a second to long to please him. He slapped his dick back and forth across my face a couple of times, ordered me to get down on all fours and stick my ass in the air. He forced me down with the crop on to my elbows with my face against the ground.

"Now reach back and lower your sweatpants Boy! You are going to feel the sting of this crop across your sweet ass for hesitating when I give you an order! Hopefully you won't do it again or you will feel the Master's wrath again when I get you home." Whack! Whack! Whack! Now, that crop was lethal. He never hit the same place twice, but after ten, I am sure my moons were steaming in the morning fog. "Now get up here and make me proud Boy with that throat of yours after you thank me for disciplining you."

"Thank you Sir for the ass whipping you gave me!" I wasted no time engulfing his cock that was quickly expanding and reaching for my gag center. I still had much work to do before I would be able to control that gag center that I had to control to get his dick down my throat properly. "Easy Boy, just breathe through your nose and swallow as it slides down. That's it Boy - much better!" Once he started to slide in and out, I got a grip on my gag center and was able to relax my throat and swallow when he instructed. It still was not a very natural or comfortable feeling for me yet, but I was at last in control of the gag sensation.

"Damn Boy, you sure do have a nice warm muscle contraction in that throat of yours! I am going to pull back now. I want you to run your tongue around the glands at the base of my dick head until I fill your mouth with my seed. I want you to get a good taste when I fill your mouth with my warm, juicy, man jizz. Don't swallow it Boy, just hold it in your mouth and don't spill any."

I did exactly what he said. Sure enough, when he exploded, my mouth filled with his spunk and I tried to hold it all in my mouth, but some dripped down out of the corners of my mouth and down my chin. He pulled from my lips. "Now swish it around in your mouth Boy and savor the flavor of your Master. I'll be checking to make sure you still have your mouth full when we get back to the house after our run; so don't disappoint me or you will be punished again for not following my orders. On your feet, pull up your sweats and start jogging around the trail and head for Lombard Avenue so I can pick up a newspaper, then back toward the house going down Scott Street."

The instant I was inside his house he grabbed me by the hair, pulled my ass up against him, ran his hands up under my sweatshirt, massaged and pinched my nipples. He was rubbing his crotch against my buns and it really turned me on, my mouth still full of his warm spunk. A big tent was forming in my sweats. He let one hand fall over my crotch and fondled, gently stroking it as he continued to harden against my buns.

"Ok Boy, turn around here and open wide and show me what you've been carrying in that pretty mouth." I opened wide and showed him a full mouthful of his spunk. "Now swallow it Boy and remember how good it tastes; you will be getting a lot of it and eventually beg for it and crave it like a good cum sucker. Now thank me for giving you a real good taste of your Master's jizz and how much you liked it!"

"Sir, thank you for letting me taste! I love the taste and smell of your juicers!"

"From now on Boy, the minute you get inside this house you will get nude and never wear clothing again while inside. Now strip, fold your clothing and pile them neatly on the bathroom counter. I'll be with you in a few minutes, just wait for me. He arrived a few minutes later in his leather harness, boots, and a pair of black leather chaps that had no crotch. His dick and balls were hanging free and swinging as he entered the room. His torso was glistening with perspiration. As he stood there, my dick began to harden just looking at his macho, masculine beauty. He stood and watched my dick stand up to salute him, smiled and stepped forward. His powerful pheromone scent filled the room and my brain went into overdrive with lust for him. He broke the mood as he spoke.

"I will show you how to clean your pussy this morning Boy, a ritual you will soon learn to do yourself each time you arrive before you can serve the Master. You must always be clean inside before you come to me from this day forward. I too like the smell of young boys like you like my masculine adult male scent. Therefore, you don't have to shower when you arrive, but you do have to keep your insides nice and clean. You also have to keep the crack of your ass clean, including your balls and dick. Never wear cologne, deodorant or other nasty scented shit. Always look, act and smell like a man Boy! Leave all that for the Twinkie Effeminate Pussy Boys!"

My mother had given me a few cleanouts as I was growing up; so, I knew what to expect. By the time he had the bottle full of warm soapy water and the end lubed, I knew to bend forward. Sure enough, he held me by the shoulder with one hand and shoved it up my Wazoo. He flipped the release lever and my insides started to fill with the rush of warmth until he emptied the entire contents into me. "Now squeeze it off Boy, don't you dare leak a drop until I tell you to sit on the john and release it all or I'll tan you hide and rub your nose in what you spill." He pulled it from my ass and shook my belly listening to the fluid slush around inside me. As I stood and waited the cramps began. He refilled the bottle as I watched. After awhile he told me, I could sit on the toilet and release. He checked the contents and put me through this routine twice more until the water ran clear and he was satisfied that I was nice and clean. He had me wash my crotch and ass with soap and water, dry and trimmed the little patch of blond hair above my dick with a pair of scissors so the blond hair was only about half an inch long.

"That should hold you for now Boy, since you don't have any hair on your balls or in the crack of your ass yet. When you do, I expect you to keep it shaved nice and smooth like a baby's ass. You got that Boy?" - I answered, "Sir, yes Sir, like a baby's ass, nice and clean too, no hair!"

"As for you my Cub Boy, you are going to learn to love hairy men, masculine men, macho and dripping with sweat and raunchy cocks, balls, head cheese, tasty asses and the taste of recycled beer. You may not think so now, but when I get you really turned on, you will beg for anything and everything I've mentioned. Just believe it Boy, you will beg for it all! Now shall we get started with today's lessons?"

"Yes Sir, but what is recycled beer Sir? He gave me a big smile!

"In time Cub Boy, when the time is right I will introduce you to everything, including recycled beer and maybe even skeet, if you're up to it! For now, march your hot ass into the playroom and make it snappy. I'm not finished punishing you for being late this morning." He smacked me on the ass and pushed me across the hallway to the playroom, one hand in my long hair, the other holding my ass tightly pressed against his crotch. I really liked his dominant style, rough and demanding.

He suspended me face down over a leather horse he had and fastened me to it with wrist locks that left me suspended, my feet about three inches off the floor. He grabbed a big paddle with holes in it and gave me ten good hard swats on my ass cheeks. I had a raging hard-on by the time he released me and pulled me down on to my feet. He spun me around and forced my lips to his left nipple. "Now service these for awhile boy, moving my lips from one nipple to the other until I had them both standing hard and erect. Nip and bite on them Boy, show me some pain Boy! Yea, that is the way you service a man's nips boy! Make em sting real good son!"

He held me by the hair and directed me to his pit. "Lick, suck, sniff and enjoy Boy! I know you love it in there, just look at that dick of yours spew pre-cum. He switched me to his other pit and I just devoured the musk and taste of him. I was mesmerized, totally lost in a surge of lustful bliss. He could see my state, pulled my head from his pit, pushed me to my knees and clamped his thighs around my head rubbing his balls over my face. His hairy balls were ripe with manly drippings and male pheromones. I licked and sucked what I could reach with my head locked in his vice grip, until he released me enough to allow me to really chow down and go wild all over his balls, cock and crotch.

He was dripping pre-cum and moaning as I slid under him further and licked from his balls down to his pucker hole. I was intoxicated, flying high on his scent and the taste of him. I was so into the taste of his rosebud that the strong scent of his shit shoot did not even register, it tasted so wonderful. He kept whispering, "Eat it Boy! Eat it! Stick your tongue up in there and really enjoy Boy! YEA, that's what I'm talking about Boy!" I just kept sucking, chewing and licking my way as far into him as my tongue would reach. Finally I just collapsed, breathless and my cock spewed my load all over us.

Master scooped it up with his fingers, and got me on all fours and rubbed it up into my rosebud, spreading it, pumping a finger into me clear up massaging my hot spot. I was so hot by the time he had three fingers working my bottom, I began to moan and squeal as a banshee in heat.

"Fuck me Master; put your dick in me! Please! Please! Oh please fuck me!"

He mounted me doggie style in one demanding lung. His balls hit my ass and he did not even hesitate one second before he was pounding my hot ass into total submission. I just automatically went into overdrive and pounded my ass back against him with every thrust. Every once in awhile he would slow and rotate on my hot spot and listen to me moan and scream out with more pleasure. He was getting close. I could tell as his dick grew in girth within me. The pressure was heavenly as it raked over my jolly button. I was on fire inside, my entire body was in flames and my cock was spewing spurts of spunk each time his dick grazed my jolly. Waves of pleasure enveloped me.

Suddenly he lunged, buried his dick, balls pressed against my bottom. He stiffened and I could feel his warm skeet spray one, two, three, four, and then five times up into my hungry intestines. I was his, all his now, totally under his control. I had spewed my juices all over the tiled floor, but remained hard and excited. His dick did not soften as he continued to pump into me again. He grabbed my shoulder muscle between his teeth and held on tightly as he worked his dick in me for another half-hour, eventually bringing us both to another sensual climax.

He pulled from me, rose to his feet and helped me in a kneeling position in front of him. "Get your tongue busy Cub Boy cleaning up the Master!" When I had cleaned him up suitably, he turned and headed for the bathroom and said. "Come along, take a shower with me Cub Boy and I'll clean that spunk out of you the old fashioned way this time so you don't drip cum for hours and wet your clothing on the way home."

He adjusted the showerhead and the spray of warm water so it flowed over us both and turned me so my ass was up against his groin and slipped his dick up into me again. As we stood with the warm water flowing over us, I felt his warm piss fill my insides until my stomach was looking pregnant. The warm fluid sent shivers of bliss through me with his arms around me playing with my nipples and sucking on my ears, neck and shoulders. He then pulled his dick from my bottom and told me step out of the shower and flush it down the toilet and return to him to be soaped and rinsed.

"Well Cub Boy, I think that's just about all the training for today." You dry off, dress and get on your way. Tomorrow morning, you come directly here by 9:00am. You know what to do when you get here - strip, clean out, and come to me only after you are ready for your training session. Be on time young man or you will get a taste of some serious discipline. Again, do not jack off or play with yourself, or I will have to fit you with a chastity belt. I want you nice and horny for training. Oh yes! You can start calling me Master Jake now Boy. Thank Master Jake for today's training session and off you go!"

"Sir, Thank you Master Jake for everything you did for me today! I promise to be on time tomorrow morning. I look forward to being with you again Sir. Bye Master... Master Jake Sir!"

CHAPTER 2

I could hardly believe that yesterday Master Jake not only taught me to deep throat his big dick, but he popped my cherry ass as well, all in one day. He disciplined me when I did not follow his orders, letting me know that he was the master and he had chosen me to be his new Cub-Boy. Yes, I loved what he did to me and was back with him the following morning letting him dominate and turn me on to him again. I had never experienced such pleasures. He brought me to a point of total submission, letting him administer a good deal of what he called Cub Boy Training. I actually looked forward to continuing with my training when he dismissed me the second day with an order to arrive a 9:00am the following morning.

When I arrived on his doorstep right on time, rang his doorbell, his voice came over an intercom system at his stoop. "Is that you Joey Boy? Push the button on the unit and answer me son, then release it to hear your orders."

"Yes, Master Jake. I'm here for my Cub Training Sir!"

"Push on the door when the buzzer sounds, come in, do as I instructed you yesterday. I'll be in the weight room doing my exercises for another half-hour, but you can come in and join me until I'm done. Be sure and clean yourself as I did yesterday. Everything you need is laid out for you on the bathroom counter." The door buzzed and I entered.

When I arrived in the weight room he was still exercising, actually on a Bow-Flex machine and smiled as I entered nude, clean and tidy like he instructed. Grandma had braided my hair into what she called a French Braid this morning. "My! My! Aren't we especially young and beautiful this morning looking as pretty as ever with that fancy new blond hairstyle? I like it Boy; makes you look even younger. The younger, the better! Come over here, suck on my sweaty body while I finish two more sets."

The minute I got within three feet of him my nose caught his scent and my dick started to lengthen and expand. By the time I was leaning over, sniffing, licking and sucking on his nipples, my dick was hard and sticking up at 45 degrees, reaching for my stomach. I let it rub lightly against his dripping torso. He felt what I was doing! "Quite the boner you have this morning Boy! Hell, get comfortable, just crawl upon me and have the time of your life rubbing my scent all over you. Come on, I know you want to do it. Don't be bashful around me boy! That's showing your Master you like him boy!" He only had to give his approval once and I climbed up on him, wiggled, and literally swam on his drenched sweating body. I thought! Did he ever have my number! He already knew from my reaction to him yesterday what his pheromones did to my libido. This was great! I was bathing my entire body against him and my dick was throbbing as it rubbed between us.

"Having fun Boy swimming on my sweaty body?" His dick too had hardened and was rubbing against my ass cheeks. He paused a moment, then said. "Really turns you on doesn't it son? Nice, it's getting me excited too boy. You are going to make Master Jake a real hot Cub boy, just as I figured after yesterday's session. You are a natural Boy, born to worship a real man, especially a ripe one!" Fuck that feels good! I do not know what I was doing, but all of a sudden, he said, "Don't you dare start getting effeminate on me, or I'll beat every ounce of the girlie out of you! You hear me Boy! I do not take to screaming faggots. If I wanted a girl I would get one!" I naturally stopped whatever I was doing after that comment. "Now get to work on those nipples as I taught you yesterday boy and do it right! That's it boy! Good! YEA, REAL GOOD!"

He continued pulling on the cables, completing his sets, grabbed a plastic bottle of lotion that was sitting on the floor and covered his dick with the solution and stroked it up so it was standing hard and ready for action. "Now ease back and slide your ass over my dick boy and work it up inside you. You are going on a wild stallion ride now while you're all slick and turned on to me. Your heart is going a mile a minute son, purring like a kitten for me this morning! Perfect time for a horsy ride; it will imprint you right to the core with a constant lust for cock! You will never be the same again! Slide back over me and get a good taste of this wild stallion's loins. A good hard ride in the saddle this morning should imprint you just fine as a Cub-Boy." I did as told, knowing I wanted to make this man under me happy, not really understanding everything he said about imprinting, what ever that was. All I cared about at that moment was getting that dick of his into me and feeling like I did yesterday again. I had craved that feeling within me all yesterday and through the night, starting shortly after he pulled from me and discharged me for the day.

I eased back over the pony and down into the saddle. "That's my boy; now start out at a slow trot for awhile until you get comfortable in the saddle. Put your feet in the stirrups so you can control your mount." He lifted each of my feet up on to a side bar on each side of the equipment so I had the ability to lift and fall over him as I slid down his shaft. Oh yes, this was what I wanted. The feelings mounted inside me. The minute he saw that I was enjoying the ride, my head back, my eyes rolling, my mouth open, he pulled me forward and held me around the waist flat against him. The pony turned into a wild stallion, bucking and snorting, pounding flesh. I knew I would loose my mount and go flying straight over his head should he loose his grip. The combination of rubbing on his dripping torso and his stallion pounding my insides was doing a real number on me. He had me screaming with delight. Hell, this was not just a stallion in motion mounted firmly to his mare in heat; it was a pile driver sinking a pier into bedrock. That fucking stallion got me off twice, then dumped its' jizz into me before he stopped and let me melt into him and shiver with delight licking and sniffing his wet mane. We came down slowly together, caught our breaths and he shook me back to reality.

"You are one hot fuck boy! Tell Master Jake how you feel now Cub Boy!"

"Oh Master Jake, I feel all warm inside, outside and I want more, lots more Sir! You taste and smell so good too sir. I could just lick and nibble on you forever. Master Jake, I love this feeling!"

"You make me proud of you boy! Now get off me son, clean me up with your tongue, and we can get started with your training this morning. I like my boys in shape with nice smooth bodies, lean, toned with nice muscle mass. I cleaned him up good, from pits to toes. My juices mixed with his sweat, a winning combination. The smell and taste was sensational, all salty and juicy. We are going to get you in top shape Cub Boy. Lay down here on the Bow-Flex like I was and we will start you off slowly to build up those muscles." He readjusted the machine and had me doing sets of about four different routines before he gave me a break. My muscles were aching already. "Hurting a bit yet Boy?"

I responded, "Yes Sir!"

"Well boy, every day you will be doing this routine for me until we get you firmed up to my liking; so get use to it. Give me two more sets." I did!

"That should be enough for today. We will sit in the sauna for awhile so your muscles can relax or you will be all stiff and sore later.

We will get those muscles working every morning boy! No pain, no gain!"

I followed him through a door off the weight-room. We had entered a sauna room, complete with a tiered bench. He poured water on a pile of rocks in the corner and immediately steam started to fill the room raising the temperature instantly. "Just lay there and let the steam relax you boy, I'll be back in a bit to join you. If you want more steam, poor more water on the rocks." It got hotter and hotter! The steam had formed a dense fog as I drifted wandering what he was doing. When he returned I had drifted off to nana land and the sweat was poring off me. I awoke to find him straddling me with his dick rubbing pre-cum back and forth across my lips and face. As my eyes focused, he said, "Slide back and sit up with your back against the wall." He scooted along with me on his knees, still straddling me, until he had me wedged against the wall. "I brought you some nice warm recycled beer boy so you don't get dehydrated. Now open wide and I'll give you a nice big taste!"

He took my head between his two palms and pushed his flaccid dick in my mouth. Almost immediately a warm flow of his piss flowed, filling my mouth. "Swallow! Drink it down boy, don't be fighting me and don't be spilling it." I knew it was useless to resist with his thighs holding me in place, his hands holding my head from turning away. Every so often he would shut off the flow, pull back, let me catch my breath, then push back in and the flow would continue. "You seem to be doing fine boy, never gagged once." He squeezed off the last two shots and his dick started to harden. As it expanded and lengthened, he pushed it past my gag center and down my throat in one smooth motion.

"OK boy, get those throat muscles swallowing and milk it! That's it boy, I know you can do it. YEA, just like yesterday! We were both sweating, his dripping down over me in the heat. I just surrendered to his control of my breathing, catching a breath when he would pull back and allow air to flow to my lungs through my nose. That taste of his piss lingered on my tongue as I lapped at the underside of his cock when he would pull back far enough to give me air. "Now swallow hard boy! Get those throat muscles busy. I will give you your reward very soon! YEA! Yea baby - just like that. Ready! Here it comes, all for you Cum Slut!" He pulled back leaving just the head of his cock resting inside my lips and I rolled my tongue around the head. My reward came swiftly - a big tasty load of his skeet. It was juicy, very tasty, especially mixed with the lingering hint of piss in my mouth. He left it there so I could suck it dry and clean! I didn't want to let go when he pulled it from my lips.

"That was awesome boy! Now, on your feet before we roast in here! He helped me to my feet. I followed him out dripping wet as he grabbed a towel and wiped himself down. He tossed the wet towel to me. "Dry off Boy!" His pungent scent filled my nostrils as I wiped my face. I just held it there inhaling, obviously too long. "Dry off boy!" I came back to earth, dried my dripping body and put the towel back to my nose. "That's enough sniffing boy, throw it in that hamper and come with me. I followed him down the hallway through a door. He flipped a couple of light switches and I followed him down a flight of stairs. It was barely light enough to see. A rush of cold surrounded me as my eyes adjust to the low light. I shivered! Light barely reflected off the black walls. This place was as a dark cave. Hell, I realized it was a dungeon, complete with every apparatus I had ever seen on the subject on the Internet or in magazines.

I looked around and realized this guy must be into some very heavy kink, the S&M stuff I had read just enough in magazines to know I wanted no part of this place. "Oh No Mister, I ain't into this sort of thing at all." I bolted, started for the stairs, but he tripped me and I went flying into the banister. I was able to catch myself and hold on without going face down on the cement floor. He had me by the braid and my arm in a split second. He yanked my head back by the grasp he had on my braid and lifted me to my tiptoes, spun me around and glared down into my eyes. "What did you call me Fuck Face? Mister indeed! Well I ain't your Mister, and I sure as hell ain't you Mistress either boy! I'm your Master, Master Jake, and Sir to you. Now, get that through your thick skull boy and YOU WILL DO WHAT I SAY BOY - UNDERSTAND!"

The tears started to flow and I was trembling. "Sir, Master Jake, this room scares me! It is dark and cold in here. I feel like the devil is in here waiting to kill me Sir. I thought you liked me Master Jake." I threw my arms around him and held on for dear life, trembling and shaking with fear.

He lifted my head, firmly cupped in his hands. Our eyes locked. "I won't let anything horrible happen to my little Cub, but this is the next step in your training Boy. I know what's best for you. You have to put your trust in me and everything will be just fine. Now stop your shaking and sniveling, I'm right here with you!" He held me to him and rubbed my back and shoulders. His warmth spread through me, his familiar aroma soothed my nerves. "Just close your eyes and breathe deeply boy." My shivering stopped and he led me back into the heart of the huge dark room. He led me to a large cabinet and opened it. He pulled a few items, placed them in my arms and led me to a table still rubbing my back and shoulders. I recognized some of the items; the others were totally foreign. He spread them out over the table.

"Let's have a bit of fun now my little Cub and see what you're made of son."

He buckled leather wrist and ankle bands with big D rings on me, attached chains running from the ceiling and floor. He pushed a couple of buttons on the side of the table. Within seconds I was suspended from the ceiling, legs attached to the floor, spread eagle, toes not quite touching the floorboards. I was pulling and jerking with my arms and legs for release. "Don't fight it son, you're my little Cub on take-off. Soon you will be flying high!" He greased up my ass and a big butt plug. He worked it up into my rectum until it popped in solidly to my chute. He attached a cord, flipped a switch and it began to vibrate. It felt wonderful almost instantly as it was working right against my hot button. I started to get excited until he fit a spiked cage over my cock and attached it firmly. The minute my dick started to harden and press against the blunt spikes I flinched with pain. The speed and intensity of the butt plug kept changing automatically, continuing to cause wonderful feelings up inside me that kept getting my cock to expand and cause pain.

While that was happening to me, he attached nipple clamps on me and suspended weights off each so when I moved the clamps caused pain to each nipple. I was moaning with pleasure one moment, in pain the next. He grabbed a feather and started rubbing it over the bottoms of my feet, causing me to pull and yank at my chains. He stopped the tickling, but attached a ball stretcher with a weighted pendulum that swung every time I moved, stretching my balls. "I'll be right over here boy watching you, see you don't hurt yourself. Just enjoy yourself for awhile while I make a couple of phone calls son. The master needs to know your pain threshold."

Pleasure! Pain! Pleasure! Pain! It continued as I hung spread eagle in suspension. I suddenly realized that the pain had disappeared, replaced with pleasure, sheer pleasure. I was warm all over and working my ass each time the dildo really kicked in and worked my jolly spot. My cock, my nipples, my balls just felt numb, but warm and wonderful too. My ass was on fire and I was moaning, humming and drooling with pleasure.

My master was sitting, talking on his cell phone, and watching me, smiling at me as I started shouting his name. "Master Jake Sir, Master Jake! Over and over I called his name until he finally finished his phone call and walked back to my side and rubbed his hands all over my sweating body. He gave the pendulum hanging off my balls a big swing, yanked on the small chains connecting the nipple clamps to their weights. I just moaned and squealed with delight, just like when he fucks me hard.

"You did well Cub Boy, take to pain just like I thought you would! Just watching you in flight turns me on son. You are a natural Cub Boy! Now I will give you your reward boy!" He loosened the buckle holding the cock cage, removed it, then the butt plug and put it to my mouth. "Clean it off boy!" I licked it clean. He left the nipple clamps and cock stretcher on me as he spun me around. He held me by the hips and in one lunge his dick buried, his balls pressed against my buns. Holding me by the hips with both paws, he swung me plunging his dick in and out over that huge veined dick, circling and massaging my little hard internal nut. "Don't you skeet Cub Boy until I give you the OK!" The pendulum was swinging wildly; the weights on the nipples were bouncing. My every circuit was on overload with lustful pleasure. I was ready to blow! It took all my effort to hold back and wait for his word. He continued his assault until he finally pulled my hips back hard and buried his dick to the hilt. He put his hand over the end of my cock to catch my skeet. He commanded, "Shoot! Shoot now Boy!" Hot juices sprayed up in my intestines as my ass muscles went wild milking his big dick. Repeatedly he shot his skeet, my sphincter muscle pulsating with my rapid heartbeat.

He stopped my swinging and fed my skeet to me with one hand as he held me tight up against him until he softened inside me. Then I felt the warm rush of his piss flowing up into me until my stomach was sticking out, looking as though I were pregnant. "Squeeze and hold it boy, you know the routine." He pulled from me, took off the nipple clamps, the nut stretcher and placed them back on the table. He lowered me back down on to my feet and removed the restraints. "There is a bathroom and shower behind that divider Cub Boy. Take the butt plug with you and clean it with hot soapy water. Use the toilet, then take a quick shower and come back here and put all this stuff back in the cabinet, including the butt plug. I'm making another phone call while you follow my instructions."

When I returned and had everything put away he motioned me over to him where he was sitting on a wooden bench still talking on his cell. He patted the seat next to him, indicating for me to sit. As I did he put one arm around my waist and held me close to him and smiled as he finished his telephone conversation. He sat the cell down next to him, pivoted around and lifted my head so his eyes looked right down into mine. He gave me a big smile and said, "Cub Boy, you made me proud today! How was it for you boy? Tell me how I made you feel son!"

"Master Jake Sir, it was the best yet. Even my nipples and my balls were on fire with pleasure after the pain went away Sir. You sure do know what you are doing Sir! I am so glad you picked me as your Cub. It was awesome Sir!" I put my arms around him and hugged him, my face buried in his chest, deeply inhaling his wonderful aroma.

"One more thing Boy before we go upstairs and get you dressed and off for the day. I'm going to put this smaller but plug in you. You are to wear it all the time for awhile. Only take it out to discharge, and then put it right back. I at a couple of little tubes of KY lotion there to take with you so you can clean it and grease it up each time you have to take it out. Remember, no playing with your cock, and be back here tomorrow at 9am. Now bend over and let me get it seated into you properly." He lubed it as I bent before him with my ass in the air leaning forward. It popped right in with a pop. "OK! That should do it! Up stairs now, get dressed and off you go until tomorrow."

Walking, especially walking up the stairs to the main floor with that butt plug gave me a good feel for what it was going to be like having that in me. I was getting another hard-on by the time I reached the main floor of the house and slipped back into my clothing. After I walked the six blocks home, I had to keep one hand in my pocket holding my hard-on from tenting in my sweats. I knew I would have to put a jock strap on the minute I got home or grandma would be shocked at my condition. Damn, how was I going to keep from shooting a load wearing this thing? Oh well, sure felt nice though, until I sat down at the dinner table that night and almost shot a load right in front of grandma. Thanks for sweats and Baggies, I could be safe from observation by prying eyes. I knew I had to walk back to his house in the morning without underwear, but for now I was doing fine, excited, but fine.

CHAPTER 3

Damn, how could it be Friday again already ran through my mind as I rushed to arrive at Master Jake's stoop by 9am? The walk without a jock or briefs under my sweats had done a number on me with that butt plug shoved up my ass. I stood there awaiting his response after pushing the doorbell with a full-fledged boner tenting my sweatpants. Then I noticed a note pined to the door. It read, "Had to leave, back in about an hour. Door unlocked. Go in, clean up, do your exercises." I thought it odd he would leave the front door unlocked, but went in and did as the note read, pulling the note off the door as I entered. I pushed the button so the door would lock behind me.

After I did the usual, getting nude, clean and washed, I got bold and went through the house looking into all the rooms. The house was bigger than I realized. I entered the master suite on the main floor. It was huge with a big walk in closet; master bath with a Jacuzzi tub a big clear glass enclosed stall shower. One full wall was bookshelves full of books and a reading table and overstuffed chair. I looked behind a big door and found a huge walk in closet bigger than most bedrooms. There were expensive clothing lined up on hangers lined up on a poll down one wall. Across from it were a combination of leather biker gear and boots. The back wall was mostly military clothing. I thumbed through the leather and military clothing and realized he must be a retired officer in the Marines. He definitely was in to leather. There were four dress uniforms with a Full Colonel Bird on the lapel and medals pinned all over them. There were just as many fatigue uniforms. I thought, "Master Jake must be a retired Marine Full Bird Colonel. I bet he can tell some good war stories!"

Sure enough, when I went across the hall and entered his office, den, computer room, the walls were covered with pictures of him and other military officers, some, obviously taken in Vietnam, some in other foreign countries, other's here in the states. There were even pictures of him getting awards pinned to his uniform by dignitaries of the US Government. There were trophies and plaques everywhere. I noticed the screen on his computer had a screen saver program running of an aquarium full of swimming fish. I turned right to that beautiful flat 19inch screen in vivid colors. I was fascinated, no, awe struck! Having an old clunker laptop, this gear was state of the art, everything, including a digital camera, scanner, cam and two printers. I was a computer buff myself. I immediately plopped my bare ass in his plush leather chair and started to scan his directories to see what he had in this baby. It was loaded with programs, even all the expensive Adobe Photo software. I then started looking at his document files. Most were on military stuff, letters, etc.

Then I stumbled upon the cream de la cream. I checked out his history folder and found he spent a lot of time on Kink, S&M, and leather sites on the Internet. I checked out the picture sub directories he had set up and found them all categorized into type of pictures. He was definitely into young boys, had pictures of him and other guys all in leather or fatigues playing sex games with young guys. Most the Cubs were from 18 to about 25. There were a few, obviously taken in Vietnam of boys much younger, all adolescents with a few pre-adolescents having things done to them by adult males, all in the nude. All of those young boys looked to be of mixed race - white and oriental or black and oriental. Some were quite beautiful, cute little tikes with big smiles across their faces, looking at the camera. As I clicked through the many pictures, I realized that all these kids were in an orphanage somewhere in Vietnam. The more I looked, the racier the pictures became. Guys were fondling, petting, nibbling and poking fingers in the little guys. A few of the pictures were of both oral and anal sex with the little guys. Even those pictures indicated big smiles on the boys' faces. It turned me on just looking at the size of the dicks on some of the guys that these kids were servicing. A couple of black guys had huge monster dicks that really caught my eye. I had heard that black guys have big dicks, and these pictures certainly confirmed that as fact. I thought, "What would something that big feel like up inside me!" I sat and admired those big black dicks for quite awhile, then moved on looking for more. I was hard and oozing pre-cum all over the Master's leather swivel chair as I completed previewing that picture folder. I cleaned up my mess with my fingers and put it to my tongue. I moved on to folders of his military pictures.

I lost all sense of time snooping in his computer files. Suddenly I felt Master Jake's hand on my shoulder. I was looking at pictures of him receiving ribbons in his full dress uniform by a General in Vietnam. Startled, I knew I was in big trouble, though he never caught me in the boy files! He never said a single word about what I was looking at on the screen. As I turned my head and looked up at him, his eyes said it all! He mumbled something under his breath and told me to return the computer to the desktop mode. When I had done that he pulled the chair back and spun it around and around until I was not able to focus my eyes at him when he brought the chair to a stop. The spinning in my head continued. He kept mumbling to himself under his breath. He then grabbed me, lifted me to my feet and gave me a quick kick that sent me spinning to my knees on the carpet. He grabbed me by the ponytail and my arm, lifted me so I was tip-e-toe. He guided and directed me with him out of the room, down the stairs and into the dungeon. Had he not a good hold of me, I would have tumbled down those stairs I was so dizzy. He was still in his street clothing.

He had me tied, gagged and suspended, dangling by my two wrists very quickly as I lifted so just the balls of my feet were touching the cold cement floor. He spun me around until I was dizzy again and my eyes could not even focus on him. He pulled the butt plug from me and greased up a monster dildo and rammed it up my ass, plugged it into that electrical connection and let it rip. Next were the nipple clamps, this time attached with electrical connections that he connected to another box under the table. He put a metal band down over my cock and squeezed my two balls into it until it fit snuggly and hooked another electrical connection to it that led down to that same box under the table. He flipped another switch and my whole body convulsed. Electrical shocks of varying intensity started working my balls and my two nipples. I never knew what was going to be shocked next or with what intensity. The pain was intense one moment, less maybe on the next. Tears fell from my eyes, as he turned and left me hanging there with that dildo working against my hot spot, went up the stairs, turned off the lights, closed the door and he was gone. This left me in total darkness to deal with my punishment and feel the pain.

I tried to break loose first unsuccessfully. Then I tried to scream and shout the pain was so intense when a large volt electric shock hit my cock and balls. The dildo kept getting me excited, but the electric shock kept making my cock go limp. Gradually I settled down and just let my mind go empty and began to hum as I did the morning before. Things began to change as a warm feeling surged through my nipples, then my cock got hard and the warmth spread to my balls. Each time the electric shock zapped my nipples I moaned with pleasure. Each time it zapped my cock and balls at the base, my cock bounced and pre-cum oozed from my piss hole. Before long I burned with lust, loving everything except the inability to stand and take the weight off my arms and wrists that were now numb. I was hard, oozing, but for some reason, I could not get off, regardless of how good it felt. I needed the Master to take me as he did yesterday. I prayed he would return soon. My muffled sounds kept repeating "Master Jake! Master Jake! Please! Oh Please Master Jake!"

I must have had my eyes closed, or out of it, as I felt hands rubbing up and down over my sweating body. When my mind registered the feelings and warmth of hands, I realized it was my Master at my side. He was dressed in his marine khakis, boots and all, even the hat with the Colonel's eagle attached. He held his crop in one hand and kept rubbing it up and down over my cock, lifting, joking, and prodding, watching it jump with excitement at his return. It still was oozing pre-cum and he leaned over, pinched off a stringer and put it to his lips. "There is quite a puddle of pre-cum on the floor here boy for you to lap up when I'm done with you today. You have been a very bad boy and are going to be punished accordingly." He turned off the electrical current to the nipples and the cock and ball devices and removed them. He also turned off the vibrating dildo and removed the electric connection, but left it lodged up inside me. I was free to swing and spin again. He started spinning me again. My ability to focus on him diminished. When I was able to focus on him again, he grabbed a black leather cat-of-nine-tails and started softly rubbing and fondling me with it. Then he began lightly striking me, from shoulders down to my ankles, both front and back.

"You like this now boy, but wait until you get a good taste of this Cat. He increased the intensity of his punishment until he was administering very harsh blows all over me. It stung more than it hurt; however, even the stings began to take their toll on me. First my skin burned, and then it seemed to be on fire. I tried to go back into a nice feeling of warm pleasure, but it did not happen for me as before.

"Oh sir, please stop! I can not take it Sir! My skin is burning! Please stop!"

"Cub Boy, this I administer as punishment, not pleasure upon your body so you will remember forever what you did without my permission today. Next time I catch you snooping, more severe punishment than this today will be forthcoming. You earned no pleasure today from me boy! Little snoops do not deserve pleasure from their Masters. Now take it like a man boy, stop your sniveling!" His punishment continued until he decided I had enough. I felt like my skin had tightened up over my muscles and was going to split open. There was not one ounce of pleasure and I was just hanging like a slab of slaughtered beef. My cock hung flaccid as he lowered me, removed the chain and pushed me to the floor. "Clean up your cock dribbles boy with your tongue!" My drippings were cold, horrible tasting off the cement floor. I gagged them down. He then ushered me into the bathroom, stood me in the shower stall and forced me to my knees.

I started to scream into my gag as he directed his cock at me. He started spraying his hot piss all over me from head to toe front and back. Words can not describe the pain as his piss covered my body running down over my reddened body. It felt like an acid bath, burning and biting into me. "That's the worst part boy! Get on your feet now boy!" He pulled the restraints, the gag from me, then the big dildo and sat them on the sink. "Shower, clean this equipment and put it away in the locker. Your butt plug is on the sink there clean it up too and put it back up your boy cunt and go upstairs and meet me in the office for your instructions."

I did exactly as he had instructed. He was waiting, still in his uniform, sitting in the big leather swivel chair I had sat in earlier in front of his computer. "Come here son and sit on my lap, we need to have a talk!" Still nude, I climbed up into his lap and leaned back against his warmth. He ran his hands up and down over my body as he turned us around facing the computer. "Now show me what you were looking at on the computer boy. Go back through all the stuff you looked at boy." My mind was churning, the wheels were spinning, wondering if I should let him know if I looked at his kinky stuff, especially the young kids in Vietnam that were being molested. I figured he already knew, probably had a program that tracked what files were opened most recently in a log. I decided I best show him everything I previewed. Otherwise, I knew I would get another session of punishment today. I repeated my basic tour of his computer. When I got to the good stuff, I could feel his dick beginning to get hard under me through the material of his uniform. He obviously was getting turned on reliving each encounter in his mind. He began to nibble, caress, and pet my nude body. His hot breath was at my ear whispering the details about each picture as I continued to click through the files. He took my cock and balls in his hand and slowly massaged until I was rubbing my ass over his hardness. Every once in awhile he would let out a low, masculine groan and his dick would twitch and throb pressed firmly between my buns. He was obviously in a world of his own as I took him back to days of each past event. Suddenly he stiffened! I felt his cock pulsate and explode against my bottom. The moisture immediately soaked his britches and dampened my moons as he jacked me to a climax. He caught my load in his other hand, then fed it to me and said.

"Those were the good old day's son! Wish I could be back there again now with my men, but I have you now Joey Schmidt! I love you son! Don't disappoint me and I'll make you very happy. Once I get you trained and use to military protocol and what is expected of you as a young marine grunt and my personal cub boy, my life will be complete again!" He turned my head and kissed me very passionately right on the lips. I felt that moment, I too loved my Master Jake, and I could love him forever, even if he was a bit kinky. "You like me boy don't you?" It was a question I had no difficulty answering.

"Yes Master Jake! I like you very much Sir, even if you are kinky and scare me sometimes! I like having sex with you, especially when you are inside me Sir! You make me feel so warm and passionate, just wonderful all over!"

"You have any friends yet your age in the city boy that you ever visit or stay with on weekends? I would like to have you spend tomorrow night with me boy, but you would have to tell a lie to your Grandma so she does not know you were here. Would you be able to do that boy? I want to show you off to some friends of mine that are coming to dinner tomorrow night!"

I only know three boys so far Sir - one next door, two further down the street. The one next door is quite young, just a kid, about 8 maybe. The other two are older, about my age, but I've never gotten too close to them yet. However, I can sneak out at night as grandma is usually in bed by 7pm every night. She takes sleeping pills and is out all night, but gets up with the chickens, around 6am. Would that work Master? I have to be home by then and in bed when she calls me for breakfast at 7am."

"That might work boy, I'll plan dinner at 7:30pm then. You call me if you cannot be here by then and make sure grandma is asleep before you leave. Be careful boy! I'll leave the back door unlocked. You sneak in, clean yourself up and put on the clothing I set out for you in the bathroom and then come join me in the kitchen where I will be most likely. I will not see you until tomorrow evening boy! Get dressed and off you go. That's all for today unless you want to sniff my pits or something before you leave."

"Oh can I Sir! Oh yes please! He opened his shirt, slipped it off and put his arms up and I turned around, sat back in his lap facing him again. We were face to face, as I buried my nose in his pit and entered the twilight zone licking, sniffing and inhaling his wonderful scent. I loved his taste today. He tasted like salted almonds." After I did the other pit and worked on his nipples for awhile, he lifted me to my feet, handed me a card with his house phone number, cell number and the code to get through the side yard gate, all printed in his handwriting. "You want me to clean you up sir; you're all messy and wet in the crotch?"

"No boy, I'll take care of that. Take this with you boy, call if anything comes up and you can't make it tomorrow evening." He patted me on the ass, sent me off to dress and leave for the day. After I was dressed and just starting to exit the door he appeared and said, "Keep the butt plug in son. I'll see you tomorrow evening then - soon after 7pm as you can get here!" He gave me a big hug and I was off.

The following morning I rose as usual. Tried to keep busy helping grandma clean the house and do the laundry for us both. When I completed my yard chores, time was getting close to noon. After lunch, I walked around the Marina enjoying the afternoon sun, feeding the ducks and wondering what Master Jake was doing. I moseyed by his house and stood across the street for awhile just yearning to be with him. I knew better, but never the less lingered for a spell before I headed back to the pond and watched the ducks for awhile. I strolled down the trail and around the "Legion of Honor" kicking stones and thinking about what to expect this evening with his friends. I just happened to run into a big black guy jogging along the trail. He was tall, black and stunning. He was dripping wet with perspiration. He had his sweatshirt off, knotted around his neck and draped down his back. I just stared at him as he passed. He was awesome. I wasn't thinking and had my eyes glued to him, especially his dick bouncing in his sweatpants as he passed. He smiled and continued down the trail. Looking at him, my mind slipped back to looking at those pictures yesterday of the black dicks I had drooled over on the Master's computer. I spun around and my eyes followed him as he continued for about thirty feet, spun around running backwards and looked back at me. He stopped and stared back at me smiling, big white teeth glistening in the sun. He stretched his arms up in the air a couple of times, then walked slowly back to me and cupped his crotch with his left hand as he stood there looking me over. He looked around to see if anyone else was coming down the trail, then looked back up into my eyes. My eyes glued to watching what he was doing with his dick, now jetting out being massaged by his huge hand. When I finally looked back up into his eyes, he smiled and gave me a head nod to follow him. He headed into a dense growth of underbrush along the trail and I followed right on his heals.

Well into the thicket he stopped, turned around, lowered his sweatpants and out popped this huge black uncut monster dick, dripping with pre-cum, sweat glistening off it, in a bush of black curly hair. He stroked it a couple of times and then stood there looking at me. He never said a word, just shook it at me, rutting from the waist. "Come on kid, this here what you white boys want! Get down here and suck this big, black juicer boy!" A big stringer was hanging from his piss hole and waiving in the air as I dropped to my knees in front of him and rubbed my nose in his coarse crotch hair and inhaled his strong scent. His pre-cum instantly attached to my chin and neck, the stringer leaving a trail down my sweatshirt. "Well, are you going to suck it boy or just kneel there and worship the beauty?"

"Oh sorry Sir, I was just enjoying your strong scent Sir!" I took one last deep breath of him then licked the underside of his shaft scooping up pre-cum right up to the bulbous head. I had never seen anything this huge, as his mushroomed cockhead appeared at this close proximity. It still had a portion of the foreskin attached, not quite pulled completely back off the glands. A couple of more licks and it popped out for clear viewing. I hesitated, just stared at it for a moment wondering if I could get this in over my tongue.

"Come on kid, I'm waiting! Do your thing Blonde!" He grabbed me by the hair and pushed a finger into my mouth, ran it back and forth spreading my mouth open gathering moisture from my tongue and spread it back and forth over my lips. The next thing I knew his dick head was rubbing dribbles of his pre-cum over my lips, nose and cheeks. Next, he started feeding his dick into my mouth, pushing it over my tongue and to the back of my throat. It was big, but seemed semi-hard, pliable rather than rock hard. It therefore curved and slid right past my gag center and down my throat without a problem. When his pubes were against my lips, my throat muscles locked and I began to swallow as Master Jake had instructed. I could feel it continue to grow and spread my throat. He had such a tight grip on my long hair I was not going anywhere by where he directed my head. He finally pulled me back, gave me air, and then plunged right back in again. He continued this slowly for awhile, until suddenly he started to increase his speed. It made my gag center waiver and my throat muscles really started to play a tune on his black organ. He moaned with pleasure, as my throat convulsed around his manhood. Suddenly he stiffened, pulled his dick from my throat and released a load of cream over my tongue. I could hardly swallow fast enough to keep up with the quantity his ejaculation was depositing. His juices began to dribble from the corners of my mouth and run down my chin. He grasped my hair tighter, pulled his dick from me and wiped it back and forth across my face. It was finally directed to my sweatshirt where he wiped it dry, pulled up his sweats and was gone like a flash, leaving me still on my knees in the dense bushes. I did notice a gold wedding band on his left hand as he left.

I knelt there on my knees for a bit savoring the smell and taste of him that filled my head. I was proud of myself to have consumed something so huge all the way down my throat. I think it was the fact that he never really got rock hard until the very last that made it possible. I thought, "What a dick on that black man, my very first too." I got to my feet and headed back up the trail feeling more lustful than ever, especially with that butt plug working in me. Thank goodness I was wearing a jock or my dick would be forming a circus tent in my sweats. By the time I reached home, my dick was pounding for release. I took a shower, let cold water flow over my dick and balls until I was flaccid, then crawled on top of the bed and dropped off to sleep. When I awoke, it was going on to 5pm, almost dinnertime. I dressed and went downstairs and helped grandma in the kitchen finish the preparations, then set the table and we ate. I ate lighter than usual and of course; she noticed and asked if I was ill or not feeling well. I convinced her I was just fine and I cleaned up as usual, as she put leftovers in containers into the refrigerator.

We watched the six o'clock news together. By 7pm, she was on her feet, destination of course, her bedroom and bath as usual. I wasted no time in peeking in on her every so often until I could see she was covered and asleep. I was off for the Masters house by 7:10, walking in his back door and cleaned up by 7:30. He had a military fatigue pant folded on the sink counter. As I put it on, I noticed it had been altered with snaps running down the sides and crotch to hold it together. A couple of quick tugs at the waistline could easily remove it in one instant. They fit perfectly, a bit tight in just the right spots, but were very comfortable against my bare skin. That was all I found to wear, except a pair of dog tags on a chair, which had my name, Joe Schmidt stamped on the tag.

I entered the kitchen where the Master was preparing dinner. He glanced over at me and licked his lips. He motioned me to come to his side and he said, "You look sensational boy - as a real Marine Cub Boy should. He was dressed in a clean Marine set of fatigues with his Colonel Bird on the lapel and another Division pin on the opposite lapel. He was wearing an apron, which looked a bit funny in that uniform. He quickly removed the apron and sat it aside. "Teddy boy, I'm going to take you in now and introduce you to my friends. They are all military men and officers, dressed similar to us. I want you on your best behavior! You must call them all Sir and if they want to touch or fondle you, you just let them do it boy. As I introduce you to each officer, you step up, stand at attention in front of each, salute and wait for him to dismiss you." He showed me exactly what he meant, coming to attention, saluting, then coming to parade rest in front of me. "Now you do it to me boy!" I must have done it right the first time, except I came to parade rest before he gave me the command. He corrected me, had me do it again correctly, then led me into the living room where four men, some older, some younger were sitting chatting.

All eyes fell on me as we entered the room. He ushered me up in front of the oldest guy first that I noticed happened to be wearing two stars on his lapel. Master Jake came to attention and said, "Sir, I present my latest grunt, Cub Boy Joey Schmidt to you for inspection!" My master gave me a little nudge with his foot and I stepped up in front of him at attention, gave him the salute and awaited his response.

The general smiled and said, "My Colonel, you certainly know how to pick out the blond beauties son! At ease now grunt, you too Colonel!" He ran his hands through my golden locks, then down over my face, neck, took me by the shoulders and gave me a big hug as his hands grasp my ass cheeks and squeezed them tightly in his palms. He loosened the top snap on my fatigues, ran his hand down and squeezed my balls and cock. I began to get hard in his palm. When I was hard, he released my dick and pulled his hand back out and commented. "Colonel, the Boy is hung very well indeed and should make a good soldier!" The general looked down at my tenting, smiled again, looked up into my eyes and asked. "Has he completed his basic training yet Colonel?"

"No Sir, he has a couple of weeks to go yet Sir! He is a quick learner, very responsive to anal play and seems to take to domination and pain well." The general pinched my nipples a couple of times, smiled at my reaction, then said, "Dismissed!" I was moved from one officer to the next, each doing similar things to me as I was inspected by them. There was the General, another Colonel, a Major and a Captain, all officers. The general was in good shape, but well into his 60's. He was very good looking too. Hell, they all were good looking, in shape and very sexy in their military uniforms. My dick stayed on hard just looking at them. The other Colonel and the Captain were especially attractive, black hair, muscled, and I found myself following their every movement. I could see a huge dick pressed against their fatigues lying against their left thighs. They obviously wore boxers. The Colonel kept rubbing his crotch every time he saw me looking at him.

Master Jake made more drinks for them and had me deliver them to each officer, then excused himself and returned to the kitchen. They took their pleasure touching and rubbing me, squeezing my ass and cock each time I came near one of them. I was eating up this attention, made a point of following the Colonel or the Captain around the room as they talked, roamed the room, picking at finger food laid out on a sideboard. Both guys had wet spots forming on the inner thigh of their fatigues. Master Jake came back in the room and told them the food was set out on the sideboard in the dinning room, as this was going to be a buffet tonight.

The General led the way! Soon all seated eating. The Master had instructed me to stand at the buffet and serve them when they wanted additional food or drink. They each knew how to give orders, and I fetched and brought them additional items as they commanded. When they were all finished eating, Master Jake told me to clean off the table, take all the food off the buffet and set it on the table in the kitchen. He joined his friends in the living room and kept an eye on my progress. When I was finished, he told me I could take my meal in the kitchen. He eventually joined me in the kitchen and we worked together putting the food away and loading the dishwasher. He never started it, just closed the door behind the mess. He had me wash up the dirty spots on the counters, stove and table, then wash up my hands and face.

He took me by the arm, pulled me to him and smiled. "You did well soldier, now let's go in and entertain our guests and see what they really like about my little Cub." As we reentered the living room he took me right to the General and said. "General, would you like to hold my little Cub, he is wearing a butt plug and really likes the smell and taste of men. He likes to be fondled Sir, but still has a feather trigger, so you will have to be careful or you could be sprayed! We are working on that Sir!"

CHAPTER 4

As the Master removed his hand from my shoulder, he said, "Go to Parade Rest Boy - spread those feet out wide, hands behind your back!" Master stood at my side, slightly to my rear and put his hand on my waistband. The general leaned forward, grasp the front. Three swift jerks, snaps released, each held half my fatigue in their hand. I was standing there completely nude. The general smiled, cupped his palm under my chin, and then ran his fingers down over my neck, my nipples, chest, stomach, to the patch of short blond bush above my pubes. His eyes fixed on my package. He cupped his hand under my ball sack and gently lifted and bouncing them in his palm, moved his hand up and grasp the shaft stroking the loose skin, watching the foreskin pull away from the head. He stopped when I was hard and released his hand.

"Step back two steps soldier boy and remain at Parade Rest!" He rose to his feet, removed his shirt and placed it over the back of his chair. He removed his webbed military belt, looped it around my neck, securing the brass buckle, creating a collar and leash. He removed his hands, leaving it to dangle like a necktie down my chest.

His hands went to work unbuttoning his fatigues, spreading the fly open wide. He unsnapped his boxers and lifted his entire package, balls and all up and let them drop before my eyes. Circumcised and hung quite well, he had a semi surrounded with the same growth of long gray hair that covered most of his chest. He stroked it a couple of times, then took a short grip on my leash and directed my face to his chest. Like my Master, he did not wear cologne or use scented soap. He smelled clean and masculine. Just a hint of perspiration was forming now, giving off his individual scent. He rubbed my face back and forth over his chest, and then guided my lips to his left nipple. His nipple was huge. The areola surrounding was the size of a quarter. As I sucked, nibbled, gently bite, he let out a moan and I felt his dick press, then rub against me. His one knee rose, pushed up against my ball sack, rubbing the coarse hair on his thigh gently against my ball sack. This felt very warm and sexy.

"Bite them harder soldier boy, show me how much you like them son! That's it son, use those teeth! YEA, that's perfect!" I realized a hint of clear fluid that tasted like 1 percent milk oozed from his nipple. Suddenly he stiffened, let out a moan and shot his load over my tummy. He dropped his knee and held me to him shaking uncontrollably until I felt the final pulsation of his dick. After he caught his breath, he scooped up his skeet off my belly and fed it to me. "Now on your knees boy - clean up this mess with your tongue!" I cleaned his stomach, cock and balls, leaving me with a powerful lust for more. I sucked his cock into my mouth and hoped it would deliver me another load, but he pulled me off and dropped back into his chair. "I'll need a breather son!" He looked to my Master. "Colonel, you have the makings of a fine Cub Boy here! He certainly got me off quickly tonight!"

"Officers, on your feet now, take off your shirts, line up here in front of me, open your drawers and go to Display at Parade Rest!" Quickly, they were all lined up in front of the General with their cock and balls pulled out an on full display, legs spread wide, hands behind their backs. He stood, walked back and forth a couple of times massaging and stroking their cocks and balls until the four were hard, including my Master. "Gentlemen, on the floor and form a Daisy Chain, show the boy how we Marines keep our pipes clean and from going crazy in the bush! Do not ejaculate!" In an instant, they were down, locked together in a circle, licking and slurping at each other. Each had a head buried in the groin of the next performing oral sex on his fellow officer. It was a sight-to-behold watching them, made me lust, wanting to be part of their action.

"As for you son, come over here and stand at Parade Rest in front of me." He dropped to his knees in front of me and buried his face in my groin. For the longest while he just inhaled, moaning and fondling my cock balls with his hands. He kept rubbing his face in my blond bush and moaning. My eyes kept returning to the display of male beef circled on the floor. They were each making the familiar sounds my Master makes when he is rutting me. I felt my cock slide into the General's mouth. His tongue circled the glands almost making me ejaculate. He felt my climax was rapidly approaching, grabbed my cock at the base and squeezed it so hard I almost screamed. The sensation passed and my juices drained back from erupting.

He backed off and said, "Don't you shoot boy! The Colonel tells me you like anal sex the best boy! I'll see what we can do to put a smile on your face tonight son! It is a Marine Officer's duty to keep his young troopers happy so they will always give their best performance when in combat! He pulled a black rubber ring with leather strapping and snap fasteners from his pocket. He worked it down over my cock, right to the base, fit the leather straps around my balls, cinched it up and snapped it in place. "That should keep you from prematurely ejaculating boy. Now go stand in the officer's circle at Parade Rest boy."

He followed me to the circle and gave my master an order. "Prepare the boy for Bottom's-Up service Colonel. On your knees men, you know the exercise routine and rotation!" My Master pulled the butt plug and sat it aside. He spread my ass cheeks, pulled a tube of KY from his pocket and lubed, inserting three fingers and spreading me gently. The other officers were rubbing and fondling my legs, thighs, cock and balls. My Master lowered me into the doggy position and mounted me as the others took other positions to massage, lick and suck on my body parts. The Captain positioned himself in front of me and rubbed his cock over my lips until I opened and in he went. Master had me grasped by the hips and was slowly entering my love canal, the Captain pushed down my throat getting me timed to his actions, the other Colonel was under me licking and sucking on my cock and balls. The Major had the largest dick, not only long, well over 10inches, but big around. He was straddle, crouched over me rubbing his entire groin, ass, cock and balls over my sweaty back. I was in hog heaven. I wanted it all and I was getting it all. The combined scent of these guys had my head swimming with their pheromones filling the room.

The General stood to the side watching, giving his officers orders, rotating their positions until I had received a load from each man up my Wazoo and a few down my throat. I was hard, excited, lusting for their dicks. Every one of them well endowed, but the Major was exceptionally large. He was prime beef, huge balls dangling between his loins. He was last to enter my bottom. As he fucked me, the General told my master to remove the apparatus on my cock and balls. The General positioned himself under me with his mouth directly under me. Each time the Major pounded into me, drops of liquid would ooze from my dick and the General would lift his head and lick it clean. The Major was really rutting me now. When the Major stiffened and shot his load, the General shouted, "Shoot Boy!" I shot a huge load and he was just in time to lock his lips over my dick and receive it all. He moaned and pulled my pubes down into his face and held me there for what seemed like an eternity.

The General finally emerged from under me, smiling, licking his lips. "His skeet is as the Nectar of the Gods men - sweet, a bit salty and a bit nutty, but absolutely wonderful! Colonel, I think this one is going to make a very welcome addition to our group once you get him fully trained in our ways. Train him well Colonel, especially in dungeon training and we will plan a party soon at my home so he can meet all our members with their Boys. I don't know about you men, but I must be on my way this evening. It was a wonderful meal Colonel, great entertainment and a fantastic dessert." After the General left, the others soon said their complements and were on their way.

"Get over here Cub Boy and give your Master a big hug, I'm so proud of you grunt. I've never seen my friends as turned on and excited with a new cub as tonight, especially the General and the Major. The Major asked if he could help with your dungeon training. You and he hit it off together right from the beginning tonight. You had something very special going on between you. You definitely have an eye for him. He would be the perfect choice for the job. Would you like that Boy?

"Oh yes master! The Major is handsome, macho, and very dominant. Like you Master Jake." I thought it best not to tell the Master I really liked his much larger dick for fear he would take it the wrong way. I wanted more, much more of the Major inside me in the future. His big dick was awesome the way it filled me up and rubbed against my special place. The last thing I wanted was for my Master to get jealous and punish me by picking someone else to assist in my dungeon training. If I keep my mouth shut now, everything will be perfect and I will see a lot of the Major.

"Come boy, it is only midnight, you don't have to get going until about 5am to be back safely in bed before Grandma gets up." He lifted me into his arms and carried me to his bed. He set the alarm for 5am, crawled in next to me and let me sniff, lick and suck on him for awhile. Before long, he rolled me over on my side and I felt him slip into me. Gently at first, then he turned wild. He roughly tore himself a hot fuck between my loins. After that display of dominant ownership over my body, he pulled from me slid down and gave me head. We cuddled and fell right off to sleep. I felt his warm breath against my neck, kissing and sniffing once in awhile during the night. I pretended asleep, but soon he brought me back to an excited state with his dick sliding in me again. I squeezed and massaged as he slowly brought himself to climax, then remained inside me and went right back to sleep. Now I was all worked up again and a bit frustrated, so I spit on my fingers and worked the head of my dick, trying not to move so not to awaken him. I dared not ejaculate, but it sure felt good for awhile, especially with his dick still lodged inside me. I got myself lusting, inhaling his scent in the bed and slowly moving my ass over his dick. Eventually I did drop off to sleep.

When the alarm went off at 4am, he hit the snooze button and brought me to life with another breathless love session. This time he told me I could cum in his hand when he ejaculated. He fed it to me, had me lick his fingers clean and popped me on the ass. "It's time for you to rise and shine Boy! Clean yourself up inside, take a hot shower, put your butt plug back in that I sat on the counter, dress and come back and give me a sniff before you head for home."

He was asleep as I gave him a peck on the cheek and headed toward home, the long six blocks. There were two people walking their dogs along my route. It was cold, soupy fog had rolled in during the night. Still four blocks from home, a police car with a single member of San Francisco's finest pulled over to the curb, gave a hit on his horn to get my attention and waved me over. He rolled down the window and asked. "What you doing out in this fog in just sweats son?" I answered, "Been to a friends Sir, only four more block to go and I'll be home."

"Well, hop in son and I'll drive you home, I'm headed your way. I just got off duty, but on call the rest of today. What is your name son?" When I told him, he responded with, "Your Grandma Schmidt's grandson then. What the hell, I live in the apartments right across from her there on Scott Street. Lived there for going on 6 years now and known your grandma for the same. Quite the lady! She bakes me cookies sometimes!" I immediately felt comfortable with him and got into the squad car passenger's seat. He made conversation immediately, said. "I just bought this Dell Computer and don't know anything about using it yet. About all I been able to do so far is play Solitaire and search the Internet. I do not have much patience with for the damn thing yet. I can not seem to figure out how to set up the email or much of anything else either. You know much about computers Joey? After I told him I had been using a computer for years and knew quite a bit about them he said. "How would you like to come by the apartment later this morning and give me a lesson or two - teach me how to email at least? I shook my head and said sure, smiled and was almost staring at his basket as he pulled up in front of the house. "OK then Joey Schmidt, my name is Officer Jerry

Gallagher and I live in apartment 26 on the second floor. Just come up anytime later this morning." I stepped out of the car; about to pull the key from my pocket that opened the security gate when he called me back. "Say hello to Grandma Schmidt, tell her Jerry Gallagher said hello." My wheels were turning, spinning having met such a nice guy, a cop and quite the hunk too. I wonder if he is married, divorced, has a regular girl. It would be great if he likes the boys. Was he giving me a good look over or was my imagination running away with me?

Grandma called me down to breakfast at the usual time. It was Sunday and she would be going to Mass; so, I cleaned up the dishes and the kitchen as usual. When I was finished, I told her I had met Officer Jerry Gallagher from the apartments across the street. She raved about what a nice young man he was and how good it was to have him living in the neighborhood. Then she said, "He is a good Catholic Boy and he goes to church; so why don't you Joey? It will make you a better person!" I pretended I didn't hear her. "You want to come to church with me today Joey? You can't go in that outfit. You have some nice clothing Joey. Why not you wear them on Sundays? You should dress up on Sundays and attend church with your grandma." I finally answered. "Not today grandma, I'll go next Sunday with you." I called the taxi for her and she was off by 9:30 for the 10:00 service. She always had lunch with friends after church; so I knew she couldn't be home until well after 1:30pm or 2:00pm.

About 10:00am I phoned Master Jake! He answered, said he was just headed out the door headed to have brunch with a couple of friends and to call him later in the afternoon. It was still cold and foggy out, but I was not going to sit in this big old house alone and vegetate. I found that old bright orange douche bag I had seen many times hanging in grandma's bathroom closet and headed upstairs to my bathroom. I removed my butt plug, filled the old girl with warm soapy water and did the deed until I was nice and clean. I took a hot shower, got squeaky clean, and replaced the clean butt plug. I put on clean cloths, a jacket and headed across the street to see Officer Jerry Gallagher and his new computer.

I rang the buzzer to apartment 25. "Yea, who's there came over the speaker?" I answered, "Joey Schmidt Sir." The release clicked on the lobby door and I entered. As I approached apartment 25, the door was open and Jerry was standing back in the room in just his uniform trousers. The belt was loose, the top button undone and the zipper down about two inches. The snap was loosened and his boxer shorts were open as well displaying a great deal of coal black bush. He was watching something on the TV, sucking on a can of Pepsi. My eyes fixed on his crotch, trying not to be too obvious that I was checking him out. The same coal black hair covered his chest and ran right down the center of his abs to the mass that covered all the way down out of sight. His pits were loaded with the same thick stuff. Even his arms were covered with a thick growth, right over the backs of his hands and on top of each finger. I thought he was handsome sitting in his squad car, but now he was more than handsome, he was awesomely handsome. My eyes kept returning to his crotch. The dark material of his pants made it difficult to see which side he was dressed. When the light from the TV reflected just right, I realized he was dressed to the left and he was sporting quite a package. I thought, "Boxer shorts are great, no support, just let it hang loose for all to enjoy!"

"Kick the door shut Joey and get comfortable. Grab a Pepsi from the Refrigerator - computers over there on the desk. Fire it up - be with you right after this WWE tape is finished. I noticed he was watching a wrestling match he had probably taped on video while he was on duty. Stone Cold Steve Austin had Jerrico pined in a headlock, just about ready to tap out. I made a comment as I passed. "Ain't Stone Cold a Bear? I did grab a Pepsi and headed for the computer. He had Windows Explorer and the Internet set up and working, but his email was not set up yet. I realized he had no document files, picture files, or anything at all in the computer; however, it came preloaded with quite a few programs and a nice Epson color printer/scanner/fax and copier combination. I noticed a couple of boxes on the floor that were still sealed. One was a Cannon digital camera with many mega-pixels - first class. I drooled! I checked the Computer specifications and realized he had purchased the very best.

When the tape clicked, started to rewind, he clicked off the TV, walked over and watched the computer screen over my shoulder. "I'll set up your email if you want Sir. Did they give you a disk or a sheet of instructions where you signed up for Internet services? He produced the disk and the instructions. I had noticed he had DSL, which was lightening fast compared to my old dial-up 56baud modem connection. After I got his email all set up and he entered his secret password I sent a couple of emails to myself, then went back in and retrieved them using my ID and password to test that it worked. I showed him how to do it all, at least the basics. He sat in the chair and he pecked out a message on the keyboard to a friend across the bay. He asked me if I would mind trying to set up the digital camera and teach him how to use it and transfer the pictures to his computer, plus show him how to scan and print photos. He pointed to the boxes and I jumped at the chance to do it. I had wanted a digital camera for some time now. Here was the opportunity to play with one. We read through the instruction on the scanner and had it working in no time. The digital camera was a bit more challenging. We finally figured it all out, got it hooked up and loaded the software that came with the camera. I took a couple of shots of him posing, flexing his muscles and acting silly. He took a couple of me. When the pictures of him appeared on the computer monitor, I maximized them, hit print and we had everything working. I said, "All you need now is some photo quality paper, some better Adobe photo imaging software and you are in business Sir. You can go into the photography business! What I would do to have a setup like this!"

He grabbed my shoulder, pulled me to him and gave me a big hug. "Hey Joey, thanks a million for setting this up for me! I owe you big time! You can come over and use it anytime I home, maybe even give me some more lessons. Damn you smell good Joey!" He ran his hands through my ponytail. "You just washed these golden locks and they smell as good as you look - a genuine blue eyed blond beauty, that's what you are Joey Boy!" He lowered his head and sniffed my hair; his nose buried right in my hair. He held me tightly, actually pulled me against him. I thought I felt his dick pressed against my side, but I was not sure until he held me out at arm's length in front of him and said. "You are one beautiful boy Joey; see what you are doing to me!" He took my hand, placed it over his crotch and squeezed my fingers around his shaft. He was growing, already semi hard. He removed his hand to see what I would do. Naturally, I caressed and fondled it for a minute. It did not take any effort to center his dick and let it poke up out of his open trousers. He went weak in the knees for just a second, and then caught his balance. He looked down into my eyes and said, "I want you, I want you a lot Joey. You ever fooled around with a horny man before"

All I had to say was, "YES SIR, AT YOUR SERVICE OFFICER GALLAGHER SIR," and I put my nose to him and inhaled. He had not showered after he came off duty and he smelled just as I had guessed he would - wonderfully masculine. His whole personality seemed to change. He went from laid back to aggressive and dominant as he ran his hands over my clothing copping feels here and there as I continued to squeeze and massage his poker. His tool was not long, about 8inches, but the girth on that baby astounded me. It seemed to keep expanding even wider as I worked it in my palm.

"Off with the clothing Joey, let me see some skin!" He assisted me, had me nude, standing before him so he could rub and fondle me, inspect my fair skin and pubs. When he rubbed his fingers over my rosebud, he realized I was wearing a butt plug. "Someone has already claimed you haven't they Joey?" All I could say was, "YES SIR, he has me in training, but he doesn't own me yet SIR. SIR, I want you too Sir!" He looked me over very closely and said, "He's already removed all your body hair, except for this little patch here above your groin. He must be military or a leather man, into some kinky stuff most likely. You like the rough and kinky stuff Joey?" I answered, "Not sure yet Sir! All I have really done so far is oral and anal sex, spankings, suspension, drank reclaimed beer, enemas, golden showers, and had a taste of the Cat-o- nine-tails Sir! I did not like the Cat at all! My favorites are strong man scents, hairy men, and oral and anal sex. I am getting use to the butt plug, but it keeps me horny most of the time Sir. Are you kinky too Sir?"

CHAPTER 5

Here I was standing nude before Officer Jerry Gallagher in his apartment, having just spilled my guts to him about what I learned to do and what I liked to do with men so far. He continued to rub and fondle me wearing just his uniform pants, his dick and balls hanging over the fly, his dick in my hand as I stroked him gently.

Well! Is this my lucky day finding you at 5am in the morning walking the streets of San Francisco in the early morning fog, living right across the street just minutes away! Today I will show you what I like Joey and you can decide for yourself if you like what I do." When I saw him first this morning, he was in his uniform, but sitting in his car. I wanted to see him standing in full uniform, packing his nightstick, pistol and handcuffs, hands on his hips, legs spread wide, chest out, sporting his nice basket in his tight pants.

I asked, "Sir, would you dress up in your uniform again and let me see you, let me undress you before you show me what you like to do?" He smiled, looked down at me and said, "Well, I'll be damned!

Sure Joey, play on the computer and I can do that for you. It will take a few minutes for me to get all dressed." He headed for his bedroom.

I sat at the computer and played, opening up the digital camera software, fiddled with his expensive new camera again, totally engrossed in all the bells and whistles it provided with its' software. I heard him clear his throat to get my attention. When I spun around in his swivel chair, he was standing there in full uniform, right down to helmet, leather belt and strapping, palm gloves, boots and the big sunglasses with the silver lenses. He had his hands on his hips and his feet spread wide. He pulled the long black nightstick from his belt and tapped it in his hand. I grabbed the camera and took shot after shot of him posing in different positions, then returned to the computer and sat down to preview my masterpieces. That is not what he had in mind to do next.

"On your feet, over here on your knees Joey boy," pointing down in front of him with his nightstick. I almost ran to him, dropped to my knees and looked up at him in total awe. I just lurched for his leg and attached myself to him holding his crotch against my face. He pushed me away instantly with his right knee, rolled me over on my back, his leather boot in my crotch applying considerable pressure. The working end of his nightstick went to my forehead, holding my head to the floor. "Did I tell you that you could do that Joey Boy? Roll over on your hands and knees, head to the side, flat against the floor, ass in the air. Stay in that position and put your hands behind you." He had cuffs on me in seconds. "Now don't you move boy!" He took his night bandit and worked it between my moons until it made contact with the butt plug and started to poke, forcing my butt plug to work against my prostrate. I moaned, "Mmmm, yes Sir, Oh yes Sir!" My cock oozed pre-cum. He commanded, "Don't you skeet boy! You have one hot bottom on you!"

He grabbed my ponytail, guided me around and pushed my face to his boot. "Now spit shine my boots with your tongue boy. Don't be whimpering either or I'll put the belt to you!" His look and the leather smell of his boots was like an aphrodisiac to my senses as

I worked my tongue all over both, top to bottom. All the time I was doing his boots he was rubbing his night bandit over parts of my body massaging and probing. It felt wonderful! When he decided that his boots were clean, he said, "Good job boy!" Now you can sniff and worship my dick!" By the hair, he lifted me upright on my knees, put my face against his groin and worked my face back and forth, over his bulging basket. The coarse material against my smooth face reminded me of how my dad would give me a whisker burn when he kissed me years earlier when I was a child. "Don't slobber on my uniform boy!" He pulled my head back off his groin, unbuckled his belt and opened his britches, his boxers and lifted cock and balls out. My face was close enough that the aroma entered my nostrils sending his masculine scent right to my brain pleasure zone. He grabbed the back of my head with both hands, fed his meat into my mouth. Within a minute I felt and tasted his warm urine filling my mouth.

"Close your lips around it boy and don't be spilling a drop. Drink! Swallow! Enjoy! You said you did this before; spill any and you'll be sucking it up out of the carpet." When he was finished relieving himself he said, "Suck on the foreskin, milk it so I don't have the dribbles. Good boy Joey!" He ushered me off to the bedroom by the nap of my neck rubbing his nightstick over my stomach as we walked.

"Well boy, you wanted to undress me. Today you will learn to do it properly, putting everything away in its' proper place." He took the cuffs off me and attached them in their proper place on his leather belt. "You can start with the helmet and sunglasses. The sunglasses go in that case on the dresser, the helmet on that stand." He sat on the edge of his bed, lifted one foot toward me and rubbed the boot along my inner calf, up slowly along my inner thigh ending with the top of the shinny toe pressed firmly up against my balls where it lifted and massaged my nut sacks. What a rush of sheer pleasure rushed up through my body giving me the emotional shivers. He read my reaction and really did a number with that booted toe that had my dick standing at attention and pulsating with the excited rhythm of my heartbeat. He then let his boot drop down ever so slowly along the opposite leg, caressing it in little circles on that most sensitive portion of my inner thigh. He had me breathlessly panting with lust, my cock drooling and pulsating by the time he had that black leather beauty stretched straight out stiff legged awaiting remove. His assertive masculine voice brought me back to earth promptly with his next command.

"The boots and socks are next boy. The boots go toes out on that space on the rack in the bottom of the closet, the socks put here on the bed." After his Boots and socks were off and placed properly, he got to his feet again. He reached out with his hand and caught a web of cock snot that was dropping toward the floor with his fingers and rubbed it over my lips.

"Loosen the clips on the pistol harness Joey." The pistol and pistol harness he removed himself once I had it loose. He wrapped the leather straps around the case and removed the pistol. He held the pistol in his right hand, the case and straps in his left, smiled and said. "This is a 38Special, six inch barrel Joey, just about your size when you are excited." He lowered it and rubbed the cold steel of the barrel against my left nipple until it was hard, then my other nipple. He rubbed it down the center of my chest, over my abs, stomach and rubbed it against my stiffie. The cold steel had me up and excited by the time he had rubbed it over both my balls a couple of times. "You like that too I see!" He placed it back in the case and sat it on his dresser out of the way from prying hands. He turned back to me again and said, "Loosen the equipment belt and hang it from the buckle on that peg on the inside of the closet door." It weighed quite a bit with the nightstick, cuffs, masse container, and other stuff attached. "Loosen my belt and pull my shirt out, unbutton it and remove it." As I slipped it off his shoulders and held it in my hand, his male pheromones did a trick on my libido. Unconsciously my nose went right to his chest and I inhaled deeply. He chuckled! "That is nice Joey, but you haven't finished what you were doing yet! Earth to Joey, Earth to Joey!" When I came back to my senses he continued. "Now hang the shirt on a hanger in the closet. Be sure to put it on the hanger so it lines up with the left sleeve dressed as all the others." He grabbed me, pulled me to him and gave me a big bear hug. "Well Joey, now the pants and my boxers and we can get down to some serious business." I worked both down over his hips and they dropped to his ankles. That scent again enveloped me. It made my head spin. He stepped out of the garments. "Drape the trousers over that trouser rack and make sure the seams are all lined up properly. Put the boxers with the sox here on the bed."

"Let's see Joey just how much you have learned and what you like boy." He picked up his boxers and put them to my nose. I just buried my nose in their scent and he could tell I liked that aroma. He sat them back on the bed, grabbed his socks and started to put them to my nose. I put up my hands, but he put them to my nose anyway and held them until I had to breathe. They smelled of his leather boots more than what I would have expected, knowing how most socks smell after they had been on feet all day. My reaction to sniff and inhale surprised him. He asked, "You like that too Joey?" I even surprised myself when I answered, "Yes Sir, it smells mostly like your leather boots, just a hint of foot smell, very nice Sir, not like my dirty socks. Mine smell horrible, like dirty rubber canvas tennis shoes and nasty toe jam."

He sat back on the bed. "Now drop to your knees here at my feet, "pointing to his feet. He lifted one foot up to me and rubbed it over my crotch playing with my hard cock and balls; then to my lips and rubbed his big toe over my lips. "Suck my toes Joey, each one individually," This was something new. I sniffed first. It smelled too of leather and the musty smell of a foot. I decided it was not bad and stared with his big toe. I sucked it into my mouth and realized it tasted better than the smell. I could tell he liked this too as his 8incher started to thicken and lift from his crotch. By the time I had sucked all ten of his toes, his dick was oozing pre-cum. "That is real nice Joey. Come up here and make love to my balls like that now." He spread his legs wide and put his knees over my shoulders giving me free access to his family jewels. The minute my lips and tongue touched his ball sack, he let out a deep-throated moan.

"Oh Joey, suck on em boy!" I alternated, not able to fit them both in my mouth at the same time they were so huge. The thick coarse hair tickled my nose, but his balls tasted and smelled so good, I could stand the tickle. My spirits were up, as was my dick as I gorged myself with their moisture and delicious aroma. I was having a little Police Ball of my own. My mind screamed lustfully - "this is what I love about men!"

He let his legs slide down off my shoulders and turned me around seated on the floor with my back and head resting against the edge of the bed. He turned around, leaned forward slightly, and backed over my face spreading his ass cheeks with his two big hairy hands. "You know what to do Joey! Show me your stuff boy!" It was dark, hairy, and lucky for me, relatively clean. Notice, I said relatively clean! I did not have much choice in the matter as his ass cheeks spread wide already pressed against my face. I was definitely repulsed until I took my first small taste. Wow! Tasted as a very nutty chocolate chip cookie when completely chewed and the combined flavor captures the taste buds. Again! This was a tasty delight and my tongue circled his rosebud, then poked and reamed. Officer Gallagher was moaning his pleasure and bouncing his ass over my tongue and against my lips. Suddenly he stopped and pulled away. "Damn Joey that felt good! Much more of that and you would have me shooting my wad."

He turned, helped me up sitting on the edge of the bed. "How about you taste a Cop now Joey Boy, see if you can get your mouth around this fatty when it is fully engorged!" He stroked a couple of times, waved it at me, then stepped right up and rubbed the pre-cum that was dripping back and forth across my lips until I opened up and sucked him in. It was truly a fatty. My fingers could not meet my thumb as I grabbed it at the base. I was able to get it in my mouth, but when it hit the back of my throat, I realized there was no way it would fit down my throat. I backed off and worked the head with my lips and tongue and it seemed to please him. His constant moaning was a good indicator of that fact. "Oh Joey, where did you learn to use your tongue on the du-lap like that; it is awesome boy. Slow it down or your going to get my big load any second. Oh! Oh! Too late Joey!

Here he blows!" I felt him spasm six times, dumping his skeet into my mouth. This was my first taste of him and it was glorious, tasted as good as he smelled. I could barely swallow fast enough to keep up with the volume. After he came back down to earth, he moaned. "Great blow job Joey!" He pulled from my mouth, jumped up on the bed and rolled over on his back.

"Joey, go in the bathroom, take out that butt plug, put it in the sink, come back here and we will see if you can get this inside you." He waved his Chubby at me! He was still at full mast! "There is lube in the medicine cabinet, bring it back with you Joey; you're going to need it, lots of it." I greased up good in the bathroom, returned and crawled up next to him and lubed Chubby up good, stroking him gently. He closed his eyes and let out a low moan. "Up you go! Sit on it very slowly boy. I don't want to tear you!" I eased down and had to put all my weight down to just get the head started. Tears formed in my eyes, but I was not about to let a little pain stop me from successfully getting this trouper to open me up. Slowly I pushed, spreading further open than I have ever been before. Finally, the head went plop, that familiar sound and I knew the head was in. I hung there for awhile until the pain subsided a bit. I put more weight down and it began to slide further inside. When the head reached my jolly bean, it must have had difficulty passing over that spot. The feeling that rushed through my entire body was sensational, half pain, the other half sheer pleasure beyond imagination. A big glob of cum oozed from my pee slit and formed a stringer connecting my dick to the trooper. He smiled up at me, rubbed his hands up and down over my sides and pinched my nipples. I settled in further. I rotated his mushroom around over my little walnut, letting it slowly move and circle that one spot. I was spewing long stringers every time Chubby poked and massaged.

"Oh you are so big around it hurts, yet it feels so good too. I'll get use to it all in me soon Sir, just be patient with me please!" I lowered myself further feeling him spread me open to the maximum, until I felt his pubes against my ass and inner thighs. I lifted up slowly and when it squeezed past my hard little walnut, my poker oozed another big stringer that floated down to his navel. I moaned, "Oh Sir,

I've never been this spread and full before! I lifted until just the head was inside and then dropped down to his pubes in one swift move. More jizz shot from my gun. Two more trips over my jolly and I was so turned on I just buried myself in his pubes and lay over on my side, pulling my trooper with me. I worked my legs out, placed them up on his shoulders, a difficult move, but once complete, shouted.

"Oh! Pleasure me! Please screw me now Sir! I'm on fire inside!" He rolled over on his knees, my legs already over his shoulders and immediately went to work slowly working my shit shoot with his lethal weapon. It was awesome! I just succumbed to the pleasure he was delivering. He whispered, "Oh Joey, you're so nice and tight baby; you fit me like a glove! I want this to last forever. Got to slow or I'm going to loose it boy." He stopped his plunging and put his mushroom right on my walnut. "Squeeze your pincher now Joey! Milk me son! Oh yea, that's good Joey Boy! Slow it down more." Each time I squeezed and milked that big head I spewed jizz, a feeling of lustful pleasure rippled through my entire body, and he let out a low guttural sound each time I squeezed. He too was obviously lusting. I lost all sense of time or reality as our pleasures continued until he again started to pump my pinkie. Gradually he increased his speed! I felt his tongue lips on my neck and shoulder licking and sucking first, and then he began to nibble and bite softly. Before long, he was thrusting within me and his teeth locked on my shoulder. I knew he was going over the edge, as his weapon seemed to grow even larger. Suddenly he thrust, pubes pressed against my bottom, stiffened, shot his skeet, causing me to shoot my load over his chest and stomach, already saturated with my pre-cum. We slowly came back to reality as he lowered my legs, lay over me licking and sucking on my nipples as I sniffed his hair.

He rolled off me and turned me on my side, pulled my butt up to his groin and pulled me up against his chest. He sniffed my neck and hair, moaned. "It's time for a little nap Joey!" This was nice, very nice, cuddled up with Trooper Jerry Gallagher, his scent all over me, my skeet rubbing off his stomach and chest against my back. We both fell asleep!

CHAPTER 6

Trooper Jerry Gallagher and I had set up his computer, taken a few pictures with his new digital camera. He aggressively seized me, molested me and showed me what he liked to do with young boys. We had more than just the usual quick roll in the hay. This trooper was a true stud and knew how to get me to satisfy a real man. As the sequence ended, he had just rolled off me and turned me on my side, pulled my butt up to his groin and pulled me up against his chest. He sniffed at my neck and golden locks, let out a low moan and then whispered. "It's time for a little nap Joey!" This was nice, very nice, cuddled up with Trooper Jerry Gallagher, his scent all over me. However, we never cleaned up and my skeet was still all over his front side and rubbing off his stomach and chest against my back. We both fell asleep together in that position!

I had no idea how long we had napped when the phone rang. When he started to lean back to grab it off the nightstand, he let out a yelp. "Ouch!" My skeet had dried, gluing his chest and stomach hair to my back. His move had pulled hair; obviously leaving some attached to my back. I could only hear one side of their conversation, but it was apparently a friend of his on the other end. They talked for just a short while until Jerry said, "Not today buddy, I'm on call and have a young man here setting up my new computer. I have next weekend off. Maybe we can take the bikes on a run up to Guerneville and stay in the cabins. I should have the new air shield and saddlebags by then. Ciao Ted!" He hung up and turned back and asked, "You awake Joey?" I answered, "Yes Sir!"

He snuggled up behind me again, lifted the sheet off my shoulder and said. "That is a nice hairy back you have now Joey; only it is black hair and doesn't match your golden locks. Not attractive at all! Now where could that have come from?" He popped me on the ass and snuggled up against me again and I felt Chubby began to lengthen and expand against my buns. "See what you do to me Joey. Feels like Chubby wants to play some more!" He tickled me and it made me jump. I tried to pull from him and escape his horseplay, but he was too quick for me and had me pinned on my back, him on top continuing to romp and play grab ass.

I shouted, "Sir you're going to make me pee all over your bed; I have to go like a racehorse." He backed off and rolled over on to his feet on the floor, lifted me to my feet, popped me on the ass and said. "Off to the bathroom with you then Blondie!" He was right on my tail playing grab ass all the way to the head. We stood side by side relieving ourselves. I watched as Chubby spewed, totally mesmerized at his beauty, all surrounded in a nest of beautiful glistening black hair. When Jerry milked the last droplets from the long foreskin, I wanted to drop to my knees right there and rub my face in the nest and run my tongue up between his foreskin and cockhead and savor the flavor. Instead, I put my head to his chest and just inhaled his wonderful scent, looking down and admiring his manhood.

"Well Joey, what say we clean that nasty black hair off your back? Off to the shower boy!" After he lathered me under a spray of warm water with a bar of soap and a washcloth top to bottom, it was my turn to hold the soap and cloth and return the ritual. I lost it totally, dropped to my knees and sucked Chubby into my mouth.

He was not prepared for my aggressive behavior and started to push me away. I would not let go, holding him to me with both my arms wrapped around his thighs. Chubby quickly gave me the advantage, taking control of his actions. He was mine now as his back went flat against the tiled stall, his legs bowed, spreading wide, letting me have full access. I rolled my tongue up into his long foreskin and circled his glands. He began to moan and slowly rotate his groin as I gathered the wonderful taste that still lingered within. I worked the foreskin back with one hand and fondled his balls with the other licking, sucking and running my tongue up and down his shaft. His knees were shaking; Chubby was at full attention, the bulbous head pulsating against my tongue. My reward shot over my tongue and filled my mouth. I just hung, working my tongue and swallowing the nectar until it became too sensitive for him and he pulled my head away. All he muttered was. "Oh Joey Baby!" His legs were still shaking and his eyes glazed over as I looked up to his face. I grabbed the soap and cleaned Chubby, holding the foreskin back to do a thorough job. I rubbed my face in his groin, planted a big kiss on the head of Chubby, rose to me feet and hugged my trooper. He kissed me on the forehead, turned me away, popped me on the ass and ushered me out of the shower stall. After we dried and I was drying my hair with his hairdryer, he stood and watched me work his brush through the long golden locks and creating a ponytail.

"You are one beautiful young man Joey! You must know that, but let me confirm that fact for you! Your parents certainly must be beautiful people too to have given you such perfect genes. Are both your dad and your mother blond too?"

"Yes Sir! My dad has blond hair and light hazel eyes; my mother is a true, blue eyed blond. Everyone says I have my mother's complexion, eyes and hair, but I look like my dad. He is definitely a handsome devil. Do you really like blondes Sir?"

"Yes Joey, I sure do son! You know it is true - opposites attract! Just look at me, Black Irish, dark, hairy and a second-generation oversexed cop to top it off. I have three brothers and two sisters." He laughed! "How's that for breeding more Catholics and adding to the number one problem in the world - Overpopulation. The pope should be proud of the Gallagher family for being so faithful to the church! What say we get dressed and go get us something to eat before I die from starvation Joey?" I cleaned, lubed and replace my butt plug and started to dress, stepping into the boxers, then the baggie pants. He watched me as the pants slid down off my hips showing about two inches of my boxers above the waistband of the pants, as I pulled the oversized jumper over my head. He asked, "How you keep those pants from falling off when you walk Joey?"

"Here, I'll show you!" I pulled a grocery store baggie tie from my pocket, looped it through the top buttonhole and then looped around the top metal button. I cinched it up just tight enough so my pants rode just above the base of my dick, twisted the tied tight and said, "See, they kind of ride on my penis in the front and on my buns in the rear." He just smiled and asked no more as he put on a nice pair of light gray tailored slacks that seemed to stretch and cling to his crotch. He pulled a purple polo shirt over his head and slipped into a pair of loafers. On the way out he grabbed a brown leather bomber jacket from the hall closet, attached his beeper to his belt and shoved his cell phone and his wallet into his coat pockets. He looked sharp, very handsome. I put on my trench coat and we were off walking toward Chestnut and Lombard Streets for a late lunch.

As we were walking back to the house, I asked him if he had a motorbike, having overheard him talking with his friend earlier. He said "Yes, you want to see it Joey - she's a beauty?" Of course, I said, "Yes!" When we reached his apartment complex, he took me straight down to the parking garage in the basement. Parked next to his patrol car was a dark blue Harley Davidson touring motor bike, loaded with shinny chrome. "Want to go for a ride Joey?" I smiled and nodded yes. He took keys from his pocket, opened a cabinet and took out two helmets. He put one on me, the other on himself. He fired up the bike, I climbed on behind him, put my arms around his waist and off we went. The fog had lifted, but it was still a bit nippy. The cold air hit our faces as he slowly made his way around the neighborhood streets, west on Lombard, up the steep hills and through the east entrance to the Presidio of San Francisco. When he reached the west-end of the Presidio, he pulled down a long narrow road I did not know even existed. It led right down to a parking area near Baker Beach on the Pacific Ocean with a great view back to the Golden Gate Bridge and across to the lighthouse sitting on the point on the opposite side of the bay entrance. He told me all this land was a National Recreation Area many call, Land's End. Equestrian trails ran through the vast area of trees, and dense vegetation, a favorite spot for hot men to walk their dogs as an excuse to be present to make contact with other guys and slip into the bushes for a bit of man to man pleasures. He said it was too large and vast for the Military Police to secure, even on horseback. We walked down the trail and I began to realize just how many men were walking the trails. Before long, we had four guys following us along the trails. As we walked looking at the awesome views of the ocean, the bridge and the undergrowth of beautiful natural flora, he talked and I listened. "Joey, this area is off limits to you if you are alone. Many a young man like you is found along these trails mutilated, beaten and dead, at least two or three per year. As beautiful as it is, never come here alone son, especially after the sun starts to go down or the fog starts to roll in." He turned back and shouted to the four guys following us. "Get lost dick heads, the lads with me!" They spread and were gone! "I just love this place Joey, not what goes on out here, but the sheer beauty of the place. I'll bring you back here anytime you want. We can bring the camera and you can take pictures. We could even have sex if you want, but never come out here without having a friend, preferably me, with you Joey! Now, promise me Joey!"

"Yes Sir! I will never come out here alone Sir! In fact, I will never come out here unless I am with you Sir! Will you take me in the bushes Sir, I am really getting turned on to you again Sir in this place?" He put his arm around my shoulder and led me off the trail into the undergrowth. He stopped where there was a view of the ocean, turned me around settled up against a large tree, loosened the bag tie and pulled my pants and boxers right down in one swift move. He said, "I like the quick access Joey! Way to go boy!" He dropped to his knees and sucked me into his mouth. I gazed out to the ocean and just floated off into fantasyland as he brought me to a quick organism. My back then slid down the tree trunk forcing his mouth from me. I kicked off my pants and boxers over my sandals, placed them aside, rolled on to my side, pulled the butt plug and sat it on my boxers. I rose to my knees, turned my head back to him until our eyes met, and began to beg for Chubby.

"Please Sir! Please put Chubby in me Sir!" I lowered my arms down on to my elbows, raised my ass and shook it at him. He rubbed my ass cheeks with his palm, lowered and removed his pants and boxers over his shoes, folded them and sat them next to mine. I said, "KY's in right pocket of my trench coat Sir." He greased me up good, worked fingers into me until I was dilated and working my ass back over his fingers. He greased up Chubby and spread my knees out further and I felt him lined up searching for the entrance. I put one arm back and my hand assisted him until he was gently pushing against my pucker. I put my elbow back down for support and his pressure increased until the head was in and Chubby headed down my tunnel of love. The pressure his girth put on my jolly button was awesome; the pain almost went away instantly now that I reamed to his size earlier today. Damn he felt good in me again! Slowly he started to work, massaging and going in until his pubes were tickling my ass cheeks. In and out, he went slowly at first. Then his plunges took on a new dimension. He pounded my buns with his groin with each revolution until I was literally drooling and moaning against the forearm that was supporting my turned head. I was looking out at the beauty of the Pacific Ocean, floating like a sea gull, wings spread in the sea breeze.

My mouth was open and calling his name as he climaxed. "Sir! Sir! Oh Sir! Oh Sir, I love you Sir!" My organism spewed from me and painted the ground, mixed with the soil of Land's End! Suddenly I was shivering as a rush of cold air off the ocean rushed in. When our bodies returned to normal, I heard him say, "Get the hell out of here you ass holes!" I looked around and the four guys that had been following us previously were standing back watching, had jacked off and strings of cum dripped from their dicks. Who knows how long they had been watching! They each quickly tucked everything away, zipped up and were off again for more thrills elsewhere. We strolled back to his Harley and returned to his apartment. On the way up the elevator from the basement, he asked me if I would give him another lesson on the computer. He wanted to know how to use the camera and print pictures. It was already going on to 4:30pm. I knew that grandma would already be home and dinner would be at 5:00 sharp as usual.

"Sir, I have to be home for dinner at 5:00pm, but I could come back later maybe and show you more things on the computer. Would that work for you Sir?" He looked a bit disappointed, but said, Yes Joey, when ever you can get away. I'll miss you - hell, I already miss you Joey. You're the best thing to come into my life in years." I wrapped my arms around him, gave him a big hug and squeezed Chubby, smiled and said, "I won't be gone long, just across the street, right over there." I led him to his window, all of which faced the street looking right across the street to grandma's house. I pointed to a particular window and said, "That is my bedroom window Sir, so close, but so far from you at night! Wish I could sleep in your arms every night Sir! Stand a magazine in the window when you are home and want my company Sir and I'll come running if I'm home." He grabbed a magazine and sat it up on the window ledge facing my bedroom window. He patted me on the ass and I headed home. He was standing in the window watching me as I walked across the street, opened the security gate and entered the house. He was still looking over at the house when I reached my bedroom window and looked over at him and waved. He held the magazine up and waved it at me, smiled, propped it back up against the window, turned and was gone from my sight.

After dinner, I cleaned up and did the dishes as usual. I finished by 6:00pm. Grandma sent me to a mom and pop grocery store to pick up a few items she needed. By the time I returned, grandma was already fixing for bed. She evidently had a busy Sunday with her friends and must have been very tired. By 7:00pm she was all tucked into bed. I gave Master Jake a call and his answering machine took my call. I left a message that I would not be able to see him until tomorrow morning. I left my email address again in case it had been misplaced and told him to give me instructions if, and when he wanted me to return. The minute I finished the message I went to the bathroom and used grandma's orange douche bag to make sure I was nice and clean again, hoping I would get lucky again at Officer Jerry Gallagher's tonight. I pulled my foreskin back and cleaned up any traces of head cheese that may have formed, cleaned my entire crotch and between my ass cheeks, dressed and ready to go. I checked to make sure grandma was OK and asleep, grabbed my trench coat and I headed across the street. The lights were on in his apartment and the magazine was still in the window. The fog had rolling in especially early tonight. It was already getting quite cold and damp.

I rang his buzzer and waited for his response. It took more time than I thought it should. I gave it another buzz. His voice finally asked, "That you Joey?" I answered, "Yes Sir - Blondie," and giggled!" His voice returned, "Well get your sweet ass up here Babe!" The release clicked and I entered the foyer and headed for the stairwell, knowing how slow the elevator moved. I knocked on his door and he answered it wearing nothing more than a pair of loose fitting knee length nylon bright red shorts with white stripes running down each side. He was all sweaty, smelled heavenly! He said, "Been working out Joey, got to keep in shape if I going to remain a cop." I threw my coat on a chair started to follow him. He turned and saw what I did and said, "Hang that on a hanger in the closet Joey!" I followed him into his second bedroom which he had all set up with exercise equipment. He grabbed a towel and wiped his face, arms and chest. "Go fire up the computer and I'll take a quick shower and be with you in a jiffy. I walked right up to him and said, "Oh don't shower Sir, you look and smell wonderful just like you are! Please don't shower!" He pulled me to him and asked, "Even when I'm this ripe Joey?" I put my nose to him and answered, "Oh yes Sir, definitely YES!" I put my tongue to his chest and licked up his sweat! "You smell and taste great sir! Raise that arm up and I'll show you what really turns me on!" He looked dump struck! I went for his left pit. He raised it up. I knew he was right handed and his left pit would be more damp and tasty. My lip, tongue and nose went wild in that pit. He finally pulled me off him and caught his breath.

"What a hot little beauty that Master of yours has turned you into Joey. He must be a miracle worker. Wow! I can not believe what you are capable of doing to a man son! You have me all worked up again doing that. How about we have a computer lesson now and see if we can cool off before you get me so excited I can not think straight. Back off for awhile Joey! The night is young. That is an order! Off with the top, but leave your baggie pants on with those sexy boxers showing." I took off my pull over as he requested. "Pull them down just a bit more Joey. Oh yea, that is perfect! That is a very sexy look Joey!" He stood and admired me for a moment. "To the computer son and fire it up. Show me one more time how to send an email, then I want you to teach me to use that camera. I want to print some of the pictures you took of me so I can send them to my mother in Sandy, Oregon. Some of the pictures you took of me in full uniform. I picked up some gloss photo paper while you were gone." We did the email, then he picked out the pictures he wanted printed for his mother and he watched me print them. I printed out a couple of shots of him in full uniform for myself. Then I grabbed the camera and proceeded to show him how to use it. He took the camera from me.

"Stand over there Joey. I want a couple of pictures of you in those pants without your top on. You look so damn sexy." He clicked off four shots. Then he moved forward, took a couple of bust shots - just my head and shoulders. "How about a couple in the nude Joey so I can put your picture up down at the precinct on the bulleting board. Maybe with your email address or a caption reading 'Hottest Ass in Town!'" I sneered at him then stuck out my tongue! He burst out laughing. "It's a joke Joey! Can't you take a joke baby? Come over here, print these up for me now and I will give you your payment for this lesson tonight." That he did! He grabbed the sides of my baggies and boxers. One swift jerk and they fell to my ankles. I stepped out of them and kicked off my sandals and I stood nude in front of him.

"To the bed with you Joey; let's get intimate and make some babies! I like to keep my bitches pregnant." He laughed again! "You know, the Pope demands this of his flock! March young man! Times a wasting!" It was well after 1:00am before he was through with me. Trooper Gallagher turned me inside out before I hobbled on home with my two pictures of him in his full uniform. What a sexy man! I knew I would be spending a lot of time with him if I had my way.

I checked to see if Master Jake had left me an email. There was nothing in my mailbox from him, just a message from my mom and dad asking if I went to church with grandma, how she was doing, etc. I looked out my bedroom window, the magazine was gone from my trooper's window and the rooms were now all dark. I assumed he had retired for the night. My ass was very sore so I left the butt plug out and crawled into bed for the night. When grandma called me to breakfast I was still sound asleep. She came upstairs and knocked on my door to roust me awake. She opened the door and said, "Joey, you all right - you sick or something maybe! Here, let me feel your forehead! No got a temperature, but you no look so good! Maybe you just stay in bed for awhile yet! Not like you to be late for breakfast!" I answered, "No grandma, I'm fine! I will take a quick shower and be down in five minutes."

After breakfast, I checked my mailbox to see if Master Jake had left me instructions. Nothing from him yet appeared on the screen. I then sent an email to Trooper Gallagher thanking him for a wonderful time and shut off the laptop. With nothing to do important today, I used grandma's douche, greased up, inserted the butt plug and decided to get out of the house for awhile. I took a ten and two five's and some change I had, my ID, bundled up and told grandma I would not be back for lunch. I headed out into the fog pointed toward the Marina. It was cold and damp, but I had layered clothing and my trench coat, so I was dressed for the elements. I also was wearing a warm, crochet wool cap pulled down over my ears grandma had made for me. I decided to head first to Master Jake's house. I rang his doorbell repeatedly. After standing there for awhile getting no answer, I headed over to the lagoon and sat on a bench and watched the ducks swim around in front of 'The Palace of Fine Arts Exploratorium.' Bored with that after awhile, I headed down the trails again thinking I may run into the Big Black Guy I blew in the bushes a few days before. No luck! All I ran into was an old bag lady I had seen many times that feeds the ducks bread crumbs, followed by a couple of skinheads that were talking loudly and giving the bag lady a bad time. They gave me a good look over as they approached. I just stepped aside, let them pass and continued down the trail and around to the entrance to the Exploratorium, thinking I would go inside if it was open. The sign read M-F 10:00am to 4:30pm and it was only 8:45am, Monday morning. I turned and returned back the same way I had walked, thinking I might still run into the Macho Black Man out jogging.

The sun was starting to shine through as the breeze pushed the fog on. That was always one of the nice things about the Marina District. The fog always lifted and the sun came through earlier than other parts of the city. The minute the fog dissipates, the blistering damp cold disappears. San Francisco definitely noted for cold foggy summers. In fact, Mark Twain once said, "The coldest winter I ever spent was a summer in San Francisco!"

About halfway back around to the lagoon, the two skinheads came out of the bushes suddenly. One grabbed me from the rear and held me as the other one snatched my cap off, gave me a couple of swift, hard pokes right in the stomach and leered at me. They were loud, obviously stoned on something, and smelled of alcohol. The one holding me from the rear said, "Would you look at the ponytail on this faggot - natural blond. Bet we could get some serious cash for it Kyle. For once, I kept my wits about me, figuring it was now or never to break loose of these dudes, neither too steady on their feet. I gave the guy in the back a jab in the rib cage with my right elbow as I poked my ass against his groin pushing him away. As he staggered back, my two arms gave the guy in front of me a hard push on his shoulders. Thrown off balance, he fell backwards. As he was falling I snatched my cap from his hand and took off down the trail toward the lagoon. I heard them shouting, "Fuck you dude we will get you next time and shave that ponytail off your fucking head too." I kept running, turned my head back for a quick look at skinheads. Suddenly I ran right into the Big Black Guy I had hoped to run into this morning. He caught me by the shoulders, held me at arm's length, looking down at me and asked. "You alright kid? Those same two try to fuck with me one morning and I show them who the man. They took off running when I got through with them in the bushes. They give me no problem since." They were still standing at a distance watching him holding me. He held me around the shoulders, walked me right back up to them and said, "Boys, this here is my Boy. I don't ever want to find out you been fucking with him again or I'll make you both my bitches too. Now get out of here before I change my mind and put this big dick down your throats again. Now apologize to my boy and get your asses out of my sight." They each said, "Sorry kid," and headed off down the trail.

He turned slightly and looked down into my eyes and said, "Well that should take care of that don't you think boy? I answered, "Thank you Sir!" He continued, "Good thing I came along when I did or they would have laid for you around here every day until they tackled you again. How those ribs feel where he poked you a couple of times?" I pushed on my lower rib cage and winced. "Not too good Sir, pretty sore!" He said, "You're coming back to the apartment with me so I can take a look at those ribs boy!" All I could say was, "Sir, yes Sir!" He was even bigger and more muscular than I had remembered - good looking too, with his big shinny white teeth sparkling surrounded by big beautiful puffy lips. His eyes were coal black; so, the whites were like a picture frame making them sparkle in the sunlight. His facial expressions, high cheek bones, shaved head complemented his toned muscular torso. His thighs were damn near as big as my waist. I looked down at his feet and wondered how he ever found running shoes to fit them. As we walked the three blocks down Bay Street to his apartment, I realized he too only lived a short distance from me, corner of Bay and Scott in another small apartment complex. It was older than most the apartments, but clean and tidy. He lived on the first floor of the four-story complex. I was quite surprised when we entered his small one bedroom apartment that there was no sign of children or a wife, since he was still wearing the wedding band. I asked, "Sir, the wedding band," with a questioning look. He smiled, held it out, looked at it and said, "Yea, divorced after 2 years of marriage. Never could get the wench to blow me, so I found out one day that white guys like to suck black dudes like me and sometimes I even find young white boys that like to get reamed with my big black dick once they get poked a couple of times. They just keep comin back for more, so I figure what the hell and fuck their sweet, tight, white asses and make em sing like little canaries swinging on my dick. There ain't no one can suck a big black dick like a white guy. Mmmm how they beg for old Amos big juicers!"

He laughed, so I did not know if he was kidding or not.

"Say kid, what's your name anyway; come over here and let old Amos take a look at those ribs for you?"

"Joey Schmidt sir! My ribs feel much better now sir!"

"Take that cap and coat off; then take off all your layers of shirts so I can get a good look at those ribs. We don't want a rib going through a lung now do we boy!" As soon as I was down to just my baggie pants, shoes and socks he gently rubbed his hands over my lower rib cage, pressing, poking and massaging. I winced as he poked a couple of sore tender spots. "I think you're going to be fine, just a bit sore for a couple of days. My Joey, your skin is flawless, white as snow." He put his nose to my skin and inhaled! Smell so good and so fucking pretty." You slide out of those shoes and socks now and off with the britches and boxers too! Make it snappy son, I'm getting a hard-on just looking and smelling on you boy." I kicked off my shoes, socks, loosened the tie on my pants, and let then slip down to my ankles. I stepped out, went right to my knees right in front of him and buried my nose in his crotch. He was wearing sweats with no support. I felt his semi hanging down his left thigh and moved it back and forth with my nose and face breathing in his masculine scent. His dick rose to the occasion until I was working a monster against my cheeks. He untied the waistband and I pulled down on the sweats until then fell to his ankles. I looked up into his eyes and he was smiling down at me. I went right back to taking care of servicing his beautiful hunk of black meat that was dangling before my eyes. Talk about awesome, just as I had remembered it from before. He made it bounce, putting pre-cum on my cheek a couple of times, then said, "Lick Joey Boy, start with the balls son, just like before!"

I caught the stringer that was dropping from the head with my tongue then went down and started nosing and licking on his huge danglers. "Chew on em Joey, makes me really hot! Oh yea! You getting me started, but nip and chew on the ball sacks as you lick and suck! I like it rough Baby! Now do that up the shaft and to the head Babe! YEA! YEA! YEA! FUCK-N-A BABE!" He pulled back, pulled the foreskin clear back, ran his fingers in my mouth and said. "NOW OPEN WIDE! DOWN THE HATCH BABY!" Like before, it was big and massive, but pliable. It bent right to the contours of my throat and down it went in one smooth stroke. "SWALLOW and WORK THOSE THROAT MUSCLES!" He removed the band holding my hair in a ponytail and rushed his two hands through my loose hair. He took two hands full of my long locks, worked his dick in and out of my throat like a pile driver, stopping every once in awhile. He would hold it completely in me, telling me to swallow, work my throat muscles more until I had to pound on his thighs with my fists for air. When he eventually pulled back he shot his entire load over my face, neck and chest, then scooped it all up with his fingers and fed it to me off his fingers. He played with me, making me reach and lurch for his fingers, as one feeds their pet, saying. "Up Girl! Get your treat! Good Girl! That's my Girl," when I would jump off my knees for his fingers. He made a game out of cleaning my body of his juices. He lifted me back up onto my feet and smiled. His dick was still semi-hard, shinny and the head only drooped slightly to the floor. It reminded me of a big black crooked banana with huge veins running down the sides.

"Well Girl, shall we warm up that bottom now and see if we can give Amos a nice taste of that sweet white corn-hole of yours?" He kicked off his running shoes and socks, then worked the sweats off his ankles and threw them on the couch. His sweatshirt up lifted over his head leaving him nude standing in front of me. He was beautiful standing there, like a black beauty, rippling in muscles. His black chest covered with little swirls of black coarse hair as covered his legs. He reminded me of Michael Jordan - the same over all look - tall, handsome and macho masculine. I ran to my pee-coat, pulled out a small tube of KY and a large Trojan, returned to him. He said, "I want to eat that pinkie for awhile before we get to that girl. You look delicious - I bet you taste like sweet molasses." He lifted me into his arms and carried me into his bedroom and dropped me on the bed, dove right in after me too. Before he did anything he said, "Don't you cum baby until I give you the ok. You will get a taste of this big black paw on you bottom if you do." He had my legs up, his big hands spreading my ass cheeks apart and his face over my balls slurping and sucking almost instantly. As he worked down over my perineum, he had me on fire inside. When he reached my pinkie and saw I was wearing a butt plug, he said, "What the fuck," pulled it from me and threw it across the room on the floor. He went right back to what he was doing. He circled my rosebud, licking and sucking it in and out with those big suction cup lips of his until I felt his tongue enter me.

"Oh Sir, that is heavenly!" His thick lips worked like a wet-vacuum sucking and pulling my pinkie into his mouth so he could actually nip and bite on my pinkie before he would force his tongue back inside and slurp at my insides. Every once in awhile his head would pop up to check to make sure I had not ejaculated. I just smiled down at him and he would go out of sight back to his pleasure. I would have let him do this forever, but oh too soon he came up for air, slipped on the rubber, lubed his cock and my pinkie as well. I was so turned on I felt very little pain as he slipped right in and bottomed out. He paused just long enough for me to get relaxed before he slowly started his assault. Soon he was giving me what I needed - a rough and wild ride on his joy stick. He became as a wild animal rutting his bitch. He dropped my legs and I attached them around his waist as he held me from underneath with his big paws and bounced me over his groin. I was letting out moans at first, which turned to little low screams. Soon he had me so turned on I was muttering undistinguishable verbiage as he licked and sucked on my nipples as he continued his rough and steady rutting. He was slobbering all over my chest and nipples when he stiffened and shouted, "SHOOT GIRL – MAKE YOUR PUSSY PULSATE BABE!" I had no difficulty doing as he ordered, as I released my firm grip around my cock and let it shoot my wad clear up hitting him on the chin and neck. This set him off immediately and I felt his dick pulsate six times, filling the rubber with his skeet. I could feel the warmth of his deposit against my pulsating pussy, way up inside. It was a fantastic climax for us both. I had thrown my head back, then suddenly forward, depositing my long golden locks down over the front of my face laid over his smoothly shaved black head and face. He just rubbed his face in it, inhaling my scent. Wrapped in his arms, we came back down slowly as I kissed and sucked on those big beautiful puffy lips.

He carried me into the bathroom still attached, lifted me off him and on to his toilet and told me to clean up my bottom as he pulled the rubbed off his dick and put it to my lips. "Drink up baby," was all he said as he put the open end between my lips and squeezed his jizz into my mouth. It was still warm and tasty, perfect for a person on a full protein diet. He then stepped forward and shoved Amos Junior into my mouth, held my lips closed around him and drained himself down over my tongue. I drank every last drop without loosing as much as a drop, ending with sucking his foreskin dry and clean with my tongue. He said, "That's my girl, no training needed!" He told me I could take a shower, but I told him I wanted his scent all over me if he did not mind. He handed me a wash rag and a towel and told me to clean up downstairs if it was sore with warm soapy water. He left the room, returned with my clothing, the butt plug and tube of KY, told me to clean it up and put it back in and get dressed. He had my ID in his hand. So, you live just three blocks from here on Scott Street Joey. I hope you will visit often. I work here in this complex full time. I am the maintenance man and manager of this apartment complex for free rent and a suitable salary. I have no specific hours, so you can drop by anytime, best to call first though so I'll be in the apartment and not out working on something. The old place is only three stories, ten apartments per floor, but the old girl requires a lot of fixing sometimes. He handed his card with his telephone number to me to look at for a minute. He then took the ID and card from me and slipped them into the pocket of my coat where he had sat it along with my clothing.

When I joined him, he was dressed, sitting in a big overstuffed chair watching the TV. I dressed and crawled up into his lap and put my arms around his neck and sniffed on him. I said, "Amos, you sure made me feel real special today, can I just say awhile here with you Sir?"

"Sure Babe, you hungry or thirsty? I was thinking of having some cold chicken, potato salad, I have left from last night with a Pepsi. You interested doll?"

"Sure, what time is it now?"

"Almost noon already; no wonder we are hungry Joey! What time you suppose to be home baby?" He lifted me off his lap to my feet.

"Dinner is at 5pm Sir; I have to be back just before then." He showed his teeth again in that big smile. "Well, in that case, get out of those duds again. We will eat something, have a little nap so Amos Junior can get his second wind and maybe I can get this big black nigger dick another piece of that hot tail before you have to skedaddle. I ain't a teenager no more, takes a while to get the old heart pumping it up for action now that I am 38 years old Joey. Some food and a nap should fix that up. You plum tuckered me out with that pretty, hot white ass of yours girl! Strip again while I get the fix-ins set out for lunch so I can just admire you some more. You are one beautiful white boy Joey!"

CHAPTER 7

"Amos Sir, would you get nude for me to admire too? You're just about the most handsome black man I have ever seen, especially when you smile and show those big white teeth framed by your beautiful big puffy lips? You're my first black man too Amos Sir and I really like being with you."

"You're embarrassing me boy, but sure if it will make you happy." He began to strip, tossing each item of his clothing at me as he disrobed, making it a game, including his shoes and socks. I did the same thing to him, catching him off guard once in awhile and hitting him with one of my items. We would catch each piece and toss it on his sofa in a big pile. We laughed and he chased me around the room until he caught me by my hips with his massive hands. He lifted me up over his head, sat me on his shoulder and carried me like a sack of potatoes headed for the kitchen. Between laughing and the horseplay, as he spun around and around, bumping into things, he finally sat me down on the kitchen counter. My head was whirling and he was obviously dizzy too, as his face nestled into my crotch and inhaled my boy scent. When he regained his footing he raised his head up to mine, smiled and put those big suction cups over my lips, sucked them right up into his and slurped them back and forth, nipping them gently with his teeth. I had never felt anything quite so intimate. When he broke away, I felt I would like him to do that forever to me.

After he filled the table with the leftovers of cold fried chicken, potato salad and some macaroni and cheese, he put one table setting on the table. He sat down, patted his lap, indicating I should sit there. I did, rubbing my ass bare cheeks against Amos Junior and he started to feed me like a baby with the one fork. I finger ate the chicken, but the macaroni and cheese and potato salad he fed to me, one bite for me, then one for him, using the same fork. Even the glass of milk he had pored we shared. Every once in awhile he would turn my head to him, looked at me, then wipe my mouth with the one napkin. When we were finished eating, he lifted me down on my feet and started cleaning up and putting away the foodstuff. We washed the chicken fat off our fingers and he lifted me into his arms and carried me to his bed. He snuggled up next to me, pulled up the sheet over us and we both were quickly cutting Z's. I awoke in his arms with him pulling my butt plug out. He sat it on his nightstand, but this time he didn't put on a rubber as he slowly pushed Amos Junior into me and rotated him over my fun button until I was working back against him and breathing hard. He took a firm grasp on my cock, squeezed it to keep me from ejaculating, and started to rut me with an intensity and single purpose - to pleasure us both. He kept whispering in my ear. "I be making you feel real good now Baby! This big black man is making you his bitch and you lovin it Baby!"

"Oh Amos, what you do to me!" This set him into lusting mode, as he pounded his groin against my bottom. He turned into a wild stallion rutting, chewing and biting on my neck and shoulders. He released my cock from his strangle hold around the base and moaned, "Shoot Baby! Shoot for Amos!" My release took him over the top and we both shared the joy of ejaculating together. As we calmed, he turned me to him; his lips fell over mine. Again, he nibbled and sucked on my lips as before. He lay doing this for so very long, then rolled over, sitting on the edge of the bed for a few minutes just thinking before raising to his feet. He turned, lifted me into his arms, carried me into the bathroom, sat me on his toilet and told me to stay. His sperm trickled from me as he filled his large old-fashioned claw foot bathtub with hot bubble bath. He crawled in and motioned me to join him. I crawled in and sat between his legs and we just soaked in the warm water together until I felt him sliding down, pulling me back enough to line me up with the head of Amos Junior. He slid me down over him again and in the soapy water slid my back up and down over him. He soaped up my cock again and he put my legs up over his thighs and jacked me as he plunged Junior into me. Water was splashing over the edges of the tub when he brought us both to a climax. He pushed his feet against the end of the tub back into the sitting position and we just sat there until Junior relaxed and plopped out into the warm water. He stuck his fingers into me and cleaned me out well, then lifted me up and our bath was complete. I dried, dressed and was on my way home at 4:25pm with the butt plug clean and again inserted to keep me dilated and ready for action.

After dinner I washed the dishes, cleaned up the kitchen as usual, I went up to my bedroom and checked for an email from Master Jake. He had sent me instructions to come to his house at 9:00am Thursday, two days from today and the Major and he would start my dungeon training. I looked out the window over at Trooper Jerry Gallagher's windows and it was dark. I went back to the computer and searched the Internet for awhile reading storied in the authoritarian section of Nifty until about 10:00pm, then readied for bed. My ass was a bit sore yet from my day with Amos, so I removed the butt plug and took it into the bathroom and washed it clean in the lavatory. Before I crawled into bed I took one last look out the window again, the lights were on in my trooper's window and the magazine propped up in the window. My heart raced with excitement! The fog had rolled in again so I knew it would be bitter cold. After greasing up my bottom well, but just shoving the butt plug into my coat pocket, I put on my sweats, my Spalding Runners, my cap, my trench coat, making sure the tube of KY was still in one of the pockets. I checked on grandma and headed for you know where. Sore or not, my trooper wanted me and I could not let him down. Just the thought of being with him again excited me as I headed out the door.

As I started to j-walk across the street in the fog, a van squealed to a stop almost hitting me. The driver's window went down and the driver shouted obscenities at me. I stepped up to the window to apologize and I noticed that the van was full of leather clad skinheads, none of which were the two from this morning. I said, "Hey, I'm sorry dude! I didn't see you coming in this fog!" I just happened to look up and Trooper Gallagher was taking in the entire incident. He waved me to get back. At the same time, the driver turned and said something to his buddies. The next thing I knew two of them piled out the side door, grabbed me and shoved me head first into the van and climbed in behind me holding me down going through my pockets. One found the ten and two fives and shoved it in his pocket, then he pulled out the butt plug and KY that I had put in my jacket pocket and held them up to the others. He announced, "Look what we have here guys, a fucking faggot and his equipment. Is this our lucky night!" He shoved the plug and KY back into my pocket. The door slammed shut and the tires squealed as I was held down and my sweatpants stripped from me.

One guy said, "You first Gill!" The other guy held me as Gill pulled his dick out, spit on his hand, rubbed it on his dick a couple of times, and fed it into me in seconds. Thank god, his dick was small, but he went at me with a vengeance. "Put the Amyl Nitrate to him Butch. It will get him really working that ass over my dick." When his partner had the Ammo ready, he had already dropped his load into me prematurely. Gill rolled off me, held me down, took the Ammo bottle from his partner and said, "Your turn Butch!" Butch positioned his body! I was not quite so lucky with him. He was twice the size of Gill and my ass already burned with his insertion. It was a fatty. Gill put the Amyl to my nose and I started to undulate and heave my ass over his dick. Having never before experienced Amyl Nitrate, what it did to me was a new experience. My head floated as on cloud nine, my ass muscles and ass went into a state of involuntary full speed and fucked his rod like that was their primary directive. Each time I would start to regain my control, Gill slipped the bottle to my nose again until my ass pumped Butch to a huge ejaculation. He said, "Who is next?" He pulled and held me for the guy in the passenger's seat. I had regained enough of my senses back to realize the vehicle was no longer moving, thinking they must have pulled off to the side of the street or possibly, we were in the Marina parking lot. I knew we had not gone to far from home. Butch said, "I'll hold him and Gill you get into the drivers seat and let Ace and Blake both back here to take their pleasure." When Ace stuck me, Butch put the Amyl back to my nose and off I went again. I drained him in twenty quick strokes.

The original driver Blake was next. Before he started on me he said, "I like to see the pussy I am fucking boys; get that cap off him and turn him over and hold his legs up over his chest. I now had eye to eye contact with Blake as he rammed his dick into me. I had an opportunity to take a good look at them all. Blake was by far the best looking and definitely the largest of the four guys in every way. His dick looked to be a chubby monster, as it filled me and then some. He took a good look at me and said, "We have a real doll here guys; what a looker. Just look at this blond hair, plus a face as pretty as a picture. Am I going to enjoy you baby! Put the Amyl to her Butch." He fucked me and I just melted into him and undulated, humped my ass under the influence of the Amyl. I was so turned on I became as a bucking bronco and he the rider. He was not a quick shooter either. He put his nose to the bottle a couple of times too. It took two more deep inhales of the Amyl before I was able to finally take him over the top and drop his load into me. He bent over and licked my face before he dismounted and said, "You're the best baby! I think you like Blake's big cock and that amyl too! I'm going to take something to remember you by now baby!" He took a knife from his belt pouch, turned my head to the side and cut my ponytail off right above the rubber band. He rubbed it back and forth over my face and said, "Mine baby, all mine now - worth a pretty penny too I'll bet!" He licked it twice and pushed it in his pocket. I was still floating on cloud nine.

I pulled him off balance toward me and planted a big kiss right on his lips. He said, "Wow, would you look at the girl go for Blake guys - must be this big dick on me! What a kisser she is too!" He took another hit of amyl and gave me another long kiss. He leaned forward and let me kiss and lick his face and lips. He loved it as much as I did. He smiled and then straightened back up. He instantly got hard again and pushed his monster back into me and said, "You want some more of Blake's hard dick - you got it baby! What is your name pretty boy?"

I whispered up to him, "Joey!"

He said, "Give Joey Boy some more amyl Butch and I'll see if I can get my gun off again before he starts to cry out for me to start porking him again!" The amyl did the same number on me and I started to buck under him. He rode me like a pro rider. I loved it! I would have let him ride me forever under the influence of this wonderful amyl stuff, what ever it was. I was going to have to get some of this stuff for myself. I kept trying to reach him with my lips to kiss him, he felt so wonderful inside me. He finally gave in to me and let me suck on his lips as he rode me to the end. Again, very long winded, Blake took a long time to shoot that second load into me. He collapsed over me and I realized I was licking and sucking on his neck before he rolled off. He said, "Wow guys, this babe is hot stuff. See if he has an ID on him so we will know where he lives for next time we're in his neighborhood boys." Butch found it in my pocket and said, "3747 Scott Street, names Joey Schmidt, 18 years old, therefore legal!"

Blake spoke up again. "Give Joey's money back to him boys, maybe she will want to service us again someday if we are nice to him tonight." Gill, who had pocketed my money, gave Blake a look to kill, but forked over the money to Blake. He stuffed it back in my pocket, gave me another peck with his lips on my forehead and said. "Thanks for the ponytail babes!" I found myself whispering to him, "Please, you come back again Blake?" He just smiled! They took me back to my address after I was all dressed and let me go.

I looked up to Trooper Gallagher's windows, the lights were on so, I ran to the door and buzzed his apartment. There was no answer, so I assumed he was out looking for the van and me. Maybe Jerry got the license number as they drove away with me and was waiting at their owner's address waiting for him to return home. I stood there thinking what I should do next when he pulled up to the curb in the patrol car. He rolled down the window and asked, "You OK Joey? I have been looking all over for that van for over an hour and a half. I could not catch the license number in the fog when they stormed off with you. Get in baby and tell me what happened!" I got in and he headed for the parking garage as I started telling him what happened to me. I pulled my cap off and showed him my missing ponytail. When he parked the car, we sat there and I finished telling him the whole story. He asked me how old the guys were and I guessed at 25. We went up stairs and he tended to a couple of bruises that were forming on my torso where I had landed on the floor of the van when they tossed me in. He lectured me on walking up to a car and talking with strangers like I did and to be more careful when crossing the streets when it is foggy.

"Joey, from what you just told me, you enjoyed what those skinheads did to you tonight as much as they did. You're all sexed up yet boy. Just look at you all hard and ready to go again. I bet the assholes did not even use protection on you! Tomorrow you will go to the clinic for testing! Now get the fuck out of those cloths before I rip them off you." I could see he was either upset that I had enjoyed myself with the skinheads or he had a bad case of jealousy and wanted to fuck me silly. He continued, "What you need Joey is some serious discipline to put some sense in that head of yours about just how dangerous it is running around fucking with every Tom, Dick and Harry you meet. There are some real bad eggs out there that would just as soon kill you for a buck as to look at you boy - dopers, smack heads, gang members, speed freaks, all looking for trouble." He ushered me to his bedroom and I finished undressing as he watched. The minute I stood completely nude he pulled a wide police belt from a rack in the closet. He stripped to just his pants and boots, put the cuffs on me and stood me up against the open closet door, face first. He lifted me up and put the chain on the cuffs over a peg on the door, leaving me suspended, my feet just barely touching the floor enough to support myself without the cuffs doing damage to my wrists. He stood back and struck me with that wide belt across my buttock and up over my back until they felt like they were on fire. Then he started back down over my thighs and the back of my calves. I was crying as he finished taking his rage out on me. He left me hanging there and left the room without saying a single word. I tried to work the cuff chain up and off the peg, but it had a big knob on the end that made it impossible.

He came back in about half an hour later and sprayed my back, butt, thighs and calves with rubbing alcohol which stung at first, but then it started to sooth the skin and ease the pain. He pushed petroleum jelly with his fingers up into me and pushed Chubby into me in one quick thrust. He fucked me like a madman; the door pounding against the wall with each thrust making a horrible sound that resonated through the room. I realized he was nude when his hairy legs pressed against mine as he continued his assault. He began to put hickey bites over my neck and shoulders as he brought himself to a raging climax with the final thrusts. I shot my wad down the inside of the swinging closet door where I was suspended. He finally spoke, "That is the way you seem to like your sex Joey so that is how it is going to be from now on boy." He lifted me off the peg, shoved me on to the bed, leaned toward me, rolled me over on my back and attached the cuffs to the metal headboard. He went to the end of the bed, pulled me down until my arms stretched taunt above my head. He attached another set of cuffs to my ankles and took one of his black ties to secure me to the bottom rail on the bed. This left me laying face down stretched out only able to roll over on my side or turn over on my back.

"That should keep you secure for awhile Joey, and keep you from getting into any more trouble tonight." He turned off the light, crawled into bed beside me, turned my head facing him and kissed me gently on the lips. He rolled me over with my back to him, cuddled up next to me and we eventually went to sleep. The hair on his body scratched and irritated my tender back making it difficult for me to sleep. Twice more, before his alarm went off at 5:00am he woke and took rough pleasures with my body. He took the cuffs off me, told me to take a hot shower, dress and come to him again before I left for home. When I returned he handed me a piece of paper with the address of a health clinic down on Columbus Avenue, walking distance from home and his own name and mailing address. He said, "This place opens at ten Joey, you be there for HIV testing boy. It takes weeks sometimes for the HIV positive to show up in your blood, so give them my name and address to send the results by mail. Now get on your knees and pray to god you are still HIV negative. You worry me Joey! Now get your ass home before Grandma Schmidt awakens!"

Later that morning, after explaining to grandma with a white lie about my missing ponytail, I spent some time on the Internet getting information on Amyl Nitrate. I had no idea how long I would be at the clinic, so I told grandma I would not be home for lunch again today. About 9:30am I headed for Columbus Avenue and the health clinic, spent more time in the waiting room than it took for them to draw the blood from me for the testing. I hoped this would improve his disposition this evening, but remembered what he had said. The long walk back up the steep streets to the Marina District was gruesome. When I arrived at the house, a horn tooted. Parked across the street was the same old primer gray van with Blake behind the wheel. He seemed to be alone! He motioned me to come to him. I was hesitant in walking right up to that van again as I did last night, remembering what Trooper Jerry had told me last night. As I crossed the street he stepped out of the van, moved around to the front and stood leaning back with his back against the grill, one leg up with his boot heal hooked over the bumper. His skinhead was reflecting in the sun, his black eyes as piercing as they were last night. He obviously knew how attracted I was to his masculine persona from how I acted toward him last night in the back of the van. He was not only handsome, but he was cocky and sporting his basket in a pair of shinny gray, metallic cloth britches I could not resist staring intently as I approached. He was dressed like a German Storm Trooper, boots, leather straps, and even dark gray stripes down each side of those britches. He was indeed eye candy. He cupped his basket and lifted it a couple of times as he smiled at me and watched me slowly approach. As I drew near, he watched my eyes, knowing I was mesmerized just watching him display his masculinity and good looks. He continued to cock tease me right up until the moment I was standing before him. He motioned me even closer with his body language. When I was standing very close to him, he pulled my wool cap off and my hair fell out, all a mess naturally. The top and sides were long and hung down in my face. The back was short where he had snipped it, some as short as one inch long. He said, "Damn Joey, you're even prettier in the daylight than you were last night. Jump in the van Pretty Boy, I owe you a haircut and then we will see how much we can get for this beauty." He pulled my ponytail from his pocket, held it up and shook it out, sun glistening off the golden locks.

"No more gang bangs like last night and I'll come with you. OK?"

"Not today Joey Boy, just me! I want some more of that hot ass all for myself!" He placed the ponytail to his nose, inhaled, stuck it back in his pocket and took his boot heal down off the bumper. He took me firmly by the arm, led me to the passenger door and popped me on the ass. "In you go - haircut, sale of the ponytail, then wild sex again Joey - in that order, and I don't want any tears reddening those baby blues when the hair goes girl, but I messed it up pretty bad last night so it is going to have to all be cut and styled." That is all he said before we were on our way over the hill, all the way south on Divisadero Street where it changed to Castro and the Castro District, the topmost number one gay neighborhood in S.F..

He pulled into a parking lot and accompanied me into a place called 'The Hair Salon.' He ushered me past the four male beauticians, clear to the back where a real flashy middle aged queen sat behind a desk looking up at him. She said with an effeminate lisp, "Well if it isn't Mr. Macho himself - long time no see Blake! I've missed your big dick coming around since Shelly quit and moved to Los Angeles!"

"Cut the shit Sugar! I'm here to see what you can do with Joey's hair, since I got carried away last night and snipped his ponytail." He turned and pulled my cap off again. Sugar went into convulsions laughing.

"Why you brute, look what you did to this beautiful boy's hair." She was on her feet fondling my body as much as she was running her fingers through my hair. "Well, let's see! As short as you snipped it here in the back, about all we can do is give him a total skinhead like you Blake, give him a buzz cut, or possibly make it short on the sides and up the back and spike the top short! Yes, that might be cute on such a pretty blond. What will it be Blake honey?"

Blake gave me a serious look, my hair down over my ears and face and said, "Hell, give him the buzz cut, high sides with a pretty little design along the edges and across the back. Try leaving the top a bit longer and see how he look with it spiked" As one of the boy beauticians washed and cut my hair, I could see Blake negotiating a price for the ponytail. Sugar was holding it and running a comb through it; sniffing it, and checking for split ends. Watching them in the mirror, Sugar kept putting her hands on Blake. He kept shoving it away as they talked. When she grabbed him by his crotch he jumped back enough to dislodge her hand. He must have said some pretty strong language to her that I couldn't hear, but Sugar got red in the face and stopped her groping and went back to inspecting my blond hair. I guessed that Sugar may have once been intimate with Blake as she gave him that look of hurt and rejection, but she didn't fondle him again. Sugar, though middle aged was a very pretty, but very effeminate. I thought, "Is this the kind of gay guy's that turns him on?"

When my beautician Teddy was finished with my hair, I felt stripped of my identity. However, he did a very nice job of cutting the hair no shorter than he had to all over. He did not put any fancy little cuts into the short hair on each side or across the back like Blake had ordered. He left the top a bit longer and it was beautifully spiked. The more I sat and looked at it in the mirrors, the more I liked what I saw, except for all the hickeys that were now visible on the back of my neck right at the hairline. This hairstyle certainly was going to be easy maintenance. I saw money pass between

Sugar and Blake, but had no idea how much green stuff he was able to stuff into his pocket. Sugar gave Blake another grope with her long fingers. He pulled back smiled at her, but immediately turned and headed and gathered me as we went to the register with Teddy and paid for the haircut. He put a $10 tip in Teddy's hand a told him he did a spectacular job on my hair even though it wasn't what he had suggested. We then headed for the front door.

Under his breath he said, "That Sugar can really get me riled the way she comes on. Oh well, once a queen, always a queen. Water under the bridge, so they say! By the way, your hair looks great Joey Baby, better than I suggested. I can hardly wait to get into that hot ass of yours again baby! Who's been chewing on you neck Boy?"

"A friend that gets a bit carried away once in awhile Blake! He was really pissed at me last night and took his anger out on me, but I did deserve what he did."

When we got to the van he said, "Now comes the good stuff baby!" He opened the side door and we scooted inside. He had a mattress down in the back and a bunch of short ropes and other items spread out on one of the seat cushions. He pulled the curtains and ordered me to strip. When he saw the welts down my back, over my thighs and calves, he said. "That friend of yours certainly did get carried away with you alright. Just look at your backside girl. You like it rough and tough by the looks of this artwork! Kinky little beauty, are we Joey."

"No Blake! He punished me because I told him I enjoyed what you did with me last night, especially my first experience with Amyl Nitrate. I think he was jealous, maybe even a bit possessive, but definitely concerned for my safety."

"Well, damn girl, I like it rough and kinky too! It shouldn't come as a surprise. After all, look at me – I am a skinhead. Looks like you may have hit the jackpot again with me girl!" He tied my hands and my ankles with short pieces of rope so I could not escape or lash out at him. He hooked the rope securing each hand up into two overhead clips, obviously installed for this specific purpose. He grabbed my sock and stuffed it in my mouth to keep me quiet. He grabbed a wide leather strap, rubbed it across my lips, then all over my body, front and back as he opened his pants and laid his cock and balls out for my view. He was stroking himself slowly as he started to spank my buns with the leather. He worked the strap up and down my back, over my thighs again until

I felt the warmth, never striking the same place twice and just enough to get my skin warm and my libido excited. He then repositioned me and did the same to my front side - chest, stomach and the top of my thighs. He was excited and cock-snot was dripping from the tip of the partially exposed head. His long foreskin still covered half the helmet and all the sensitive glands surrounding the huge mushroom. He said, "Looks to me like you like the strap girl." He took my hard dick in his hand and squeezed it a few times as pre-cum oozed from my cock too.

"Let's see how you hold up under severe nipple play girl!" He put his mouth to my nipples, sucked, chewed, and tweaked them for awhile. Once he had me moaning with pleasure, he began to really nip and bite them. He got down right mean with those pearly whites of his. He grabbed the Amyl and put it to my nose, took a hit himself and went right back to biting my nipples as he rubbed his hard dick against my thigh. He reached up and released the clips from my wrists and I fell back onto the mattress. He stripped completely knowing I was watching every piece of his wardrobe separate from his body. It was awesome watching this striptease as his magnificently sculptured body came into full view to me for the first time. He was quickly all over me licking, sucking, biting - ears, neck, even my armpits after he gave us both another hit on the Amyl. Blake rubbed and crawled over me licking and biting every sensitive area on my upper body. He sat up on his butt, pulled my ass up to his groin facing him, lifted my ass up and hooked my leg ties to the two clips. This suspended me so he could bury his face in my groin with my legs up in the air and his dick pressed against my back. He gave us both another big hit on the amyl and wiggled himself down under me enough so he had total access with his tongue to my pinkie. He went wild sucking and chewing.

I was humping my ass over his tongue and lips moaning, "Oh Blake – Yes, Yes, suck me!" He was humping my back spreading pre-cum drooling from his manhood all over my back, allowing me to slip and slide over his monster dick. He licked, sucked and opened me up. I wanted him inside me now more than ever. I lusted for that feel again.

I whimpered, "Fuck me Blake! Please fuck me!" That was his cue! He knew I was ready! His hands went up and released my ankles from the clips and my legs came down over him. He pulled me up into his lap and worked his huge dripping appendage into me and I began to ride him. More amyl to both of us and I was bouncing like a jack-in-the-box. We were both breathless as he popped his cookie and my juices also covered his chest and stomach. He held me to him, we rolled over and readjusted with my legs up over his shoulders and he went at me again without even softening. Each time he put the amyl to my nose I rocketed and my insides and ass automatically vibrated and milked as if they had a mind of their own. He just held still and let me turn loose on him as he leaned over me, chewing and sucking on my nipples. Occasionally he slapped my ass when my undulations would slow. He would give me another hit of the amyl and my rutting continued. Wanting this to last forever, I just molded to him and let him chew and bite all over the body parts he could reach with his powerful jaws and suctioning lips. I knew I would have more hickeys all over the front of me, but I did not care, he was giving me such pleasure. Eventually, as everything, it had to cum-to-an-end, with another massive ejaculation into my bottom and more of my skeet over my stomach.

He lowered my legs, rolled over on his back and said. "Clean up the mess with your tongue baby. Do a good job too or you will get another taste of the strap!" When I was all done and we were dressed, he drove me back to the house. He pulled across the street at the same spot he parked earlier. He grabbed my thigh, gave it a squeeze and said, "Tomorrow morning girl! You be out here at 10:00am and do not be late! Oh yea, here is half the money I negotiated out of Sugar for your ponytail." He opened the roll of money he pulled from his pocket, counted out $150 into my palm. I was amazed! It must have showed in my eyes too. He said, "Well! Natural blond 18 inches long, about $16.50 per inch. I tried for $20 per inch, but Sugar is a tough negotiator. Probably could have gotten more somewhere else, but that is not too bad a price. I have to get going now Joey, see you in the morning!"

As I entered the house and grandma saw my hair, her arm went out to me and she hugged me to her. "Oh Joey, you look so good. I like! You look like a boy now Joey! Grandma is proud of you Joey - my handsome boy!" I thought to myself, "If she only knew - if she only knew!"

CHAPTER 8

Here it was only 3:00pm Tuesday afternoon. I had already been to the Health Clinic, received a buzz haircut, and had wild sex with Blake in the back of his van. To top it off, he had handed me half the profit from the sale of my ponytail, $150. I kept pulling up my sweatshirt and putting it to my nose. It had the wonderful smell of Blake all over it, as did I. Damn he smelled good! I hated to take a bath. However, I knew I best or later today Trooper Jerry would really put the belt to me more harshly than he did last night if I had another man's scent on me. I used 'Big Orange' to clean my shit chute and then jumped into a hot bath. I must have soaked in the tube for an hour. As I dried, I looked in the mirror wondering how I was going to camouflage all the new hickeys and marks down my front side that Blake had added to me earlier today. I rummaged through the drawers and dressers of the spare bedroom and bathroom hoping to come up with some of mom's makeup somewhere. Her skin tone was about the same shade as mine. I lucked out - found a bottle of liquid makeup base and a bottle of light blush. Mixing a bit of each bottle, I was able to make a blend that was perfect to do the job. I only covered the skin damaged by Blake's lips, teeth and the strap down my front side. The others I left alone.

After a short nap, then dinner, I watched TV with grandma for awhile, then went up to my bedroom and checked for any emails, read a couple of stories I had been following on Nifty. I kept checking to see if the lights were on yet in Trooper's windows. At 10:30pm the lights were on and his belt was hanging in the window. That gave me an idea of what to expect from him tonight! I greased up my bottom well and inserted the butt plug, dressed in boxers, a very large pair of baggie pants, a Lakers' Jersey, a pair of long sweat socks, and my runners. I checked on sleeping grandma, grabbed my cap, coat, and started to head out. Then, all of a sudden it dawned on me that the Trooper would want to see proof that I went to the clinic that morning. I dug in the coat pocket and found the receipt and a couple of pamphlets and some written material on HIV+ and AIDS. I stuffed it all back into my coat pocket and off I went. I was very careful to look both ways in the fog before I crossed the street. Trooper Jerry Gallagher buzzed me in and as I entered the apartment I found him still dressed in his full uniform. He looked mouth watering delicious in that uniform. He put his hand out, "You bring anything from the clinic Joey?" I answered, "Yes Sir!" I emptied my pockets of all the paperwork and literature they had given me. He took it all from me, looked through it all until he found the receipt. It checked it out and then handed it back to me to put back in my coat pockets.

"Joey I want you to read all that literature. I found out just today myself that this deadly virus sometimes could take weeks, even months to show up in your blood samples after initial contact. Any initial test report could show you HIV negative today, but AIDS doesn't work that way baby! The antibodies can take weeks, even months to show up in your body, and that is what the HIV testing is all about. Just because you may test negative today does not mean you are not infected.

Tomorrow, a week, or four months from now testing could prove you HIV positive. The damn initial reports that classify a patient as HIV negative give the patient a false sense of hope that they are not infected. That's why you are going to get tested every week for at least two months, then at least once a month after that. I am surprised you and countless other teens do not know more about the AIDS virus today and are not always practicing safe sex. Too many people are getting sick and dying, simply because they did not know better! Now that I have explained this to you Joey, you know, and I do not want you ever again to have sex without protection. That is an order boy!"

"Now, hang your coat and cap up in the closet and get over here and let me get a good look at you in that Lakers' Jersey and those baggy pants hanging low off your round, cute ass. You are one living doll Joey - young and beautiful - way too beautiful to die of a deadly virus like AIDS like countless others like you have these past few years! In fact, my next day off I am taking you to a hospital ward at UC Hospital so you can get a first hand view of boys your age now with full blown AIDS. That should cool your whoring around boy!" I took the coat off first and hung it on a hanger in the closet, knowing he was watching me. I turned and faced him and slowly removed the wool cap to see the expression on his face when he got a look at my new haircut. His eyes lit up into a big smile as he took two giant steps in his big black boots to me. He threw one arm around my neck in a headlock and gave me a Burnie with his knuckles on the top of my head. He then turned me around and around a couple of times looking at the spikes across the top. All he said was, "Fantastic!" He did something that surprised me. He laid me out flat on my back on the carpet, lay flat over me and rutted me until his dick was hard, bulging against me. We were both fully clothed. He began to lick and slurp all over my face, my neck and nibble on my ear. Eventually he rose straddle me on his knees and removed my Lakers' Jersey, leaned back and pulled off both my runners and socks. He loomed over me fully clothed in his trooper uniform yet, pulled his belt off and rubbed it back and forth across my lips for a moment before setting it off to the side.

He opened his britches, scooped Chubby and his danglers out, rubbed them over my chin, lips and face. He used his fingers to open and explore my mouth, holding it open as he worked the belt behind my head. He grabbed the belt by each end and lifted supporting my head. He pumped my head up and down with that belt, working my mouth over his manhood. My head was in the leather sling, both his hands clasp on the belt pulling my face into his groin. He mixed that action with thrusts from his crotch. Chubby was trying to enter my throat, but seemed too large to enter. He finally lifted my head with such a force at a new angle that Chubby opened up the passageway and slid down my throat, causing me to convulse and gag. He held me firmly in place as I pounded on his thighs for release. He finally eased my head just enough so I could inhale much needed oxygen into my lungs, and immediately pulled my head back over Chubby. A few more trips down the hatch, and I was able to get into the steady rhythm he created until he stiffened and shot his load, barely giving me a taste as he lifted my head back up for air. Only a few dribbles of his load remained on Chubby to give me a taste over my tongue. My head dropped to the carpet. He rose to his feet and stared down at me and said, "We got Chubby down the hatch boy, now we know he fits perfectly! Be easier next time now that we opened your tight throat up officially for business. Get on your feet boy!" My throat was sore, raw and I was pissed big time! My throat was on fire from his assault, throbbing actually.

I tried to shout at him, but my voice box seemed paralyzed. Nothing came out! This further irritated me, so I kicked out at him with my bare foot, aiming for his groin. He saw it coming, grabbed my bare foot and I went in the air, then to my back against the carpet. Laughing, he stepped forward, put his boot on my bare chest and said, "Get use to it Joey, Chubby liked your tight throat and will be in there a lot in the future baby! He might even lower your voice an octave - from a tenor to a baritone!" I lashed out at him again with my fists, pounding on his leg. "Oh good, Joey's all fired up and full of spunk tonight. This is my lucky night alright!" He took the loose belt in his hand, wrapped it around my neck making a collar and leash. He removed his boot from my chest and lifted me up into the seated position. "Over on all fours!" The minute I was on all fours, he snapped on the leash and said. "Heel bitch," tugged on the leash, forced me to keep up with him as he pranced around the room, his cock and balls bouncing from his open trousers. Good thing I still had on my Baggies or I would have had carpet burns on my knees when he finally came to a stop on the tiled floor of the bathroom. I was out of breath, heart pounding, and sweating profusely by now.

"By the looks of you bitch, we better get some liquid into you so you don't get all dehydrated. Sit girl, sit up and open wide!" He fed Chubby into my mouth! Soon I felt the flow going over my tongue and down as I gobbled and swallowed his warm liquid. "Now suck the skin nice and dry! That's a good girl!" He patted my head, and said, "On your feet now Joey," leaving the collar and leash dangling from my neck. With some effort, I was able to get to my feet and stand before him. He leaned forward, licked some sweat from my nipple and smiled. "My little bitch even tastes good tonight! Turn around and let me take a good look at your backside and those welts I put on you last night." He ran his hands over my back. "Lower the pants now girl." He continued, running his hands over my ass, down the back of my thighs, calves and again to my ass. He gave them another couple of squeezes. "You are OK, looking fine girl! Pull up your boxers and britches now Joey and follow me. I have something to show you babe!"

When he stopped in the bedroom, he pointed to the wall. He had framed the pictures he took of me in just my boxers and baggie pants, and the two shots of just my face, hair and shoulders. He had them hanging on the wall next to a couple of him with his shirt off in his uniform pants and boots, all in matching black frames. "My little bitch and her big daddy – you like?" I was impressed, he had them matted and they looked great, in living color. I answered, "Beautiful job Sir, you are one hot dude in or out of uniform."

"Well Joey, looks like Chubby is stirring again! Drop those britches boy! You are going on the peg again son, just like last night. I'm going to pound that sweet ass of yours' again boy, until you put another load of cum down the closet door to match the one dried there already." He cuffed me and hung me, put his arms around me and removed the plastic tie holding my pants up and yanked my baggies and boxers down. He kicked them to the side and fondled me top to bottom, eventually pulling the butt plug and rubbing Chubby up and down in the crack of my ass. One lunge and he buried in me and the door banged against the wall with a thud. He must have liked that pounding sound, as he pounded out a base drum solo with his continued thrusts, all in rhythm. He slowed enough to remove some of his gear and open his shirt so his bare chest rubbed against my back. He then started to pound out a beat that slowly increased until it was a fast rap beat accompanying his lustful moans and masculine rutting sounds. When I started to cream the door, it took him over the edge and he stiffened and enjoyed my special muscle contractions on Chubby, shooting spasm after spasm of skeet into me.

He pulled from me, leaving me hang there and left the room for awhile. His skeet was running down my inner thighs and legs when he returned. He noticed and smacked me on the ass a couple of times and said, "Tighten up your ass girl - you are dripping on the carpet." He grabbed the belt again and started on me - just the ass cheeks this time. He left the room again and returned with a towel. He wiped up the mess on the carpet, leaving the towel in place to catch any additional dripping. "Let it drip now girl! You will just hang there to drip dry for awhile for dripping on my carpet. Your ass sure is pretty all pink like that baby!" He put his hand on my buns. "Nice and warm too Joey Baby, making Chubby stir a bit! Look around here son, what that warm pink ass of yours is doing to old Chubby!" I turned my head to the side and Chubby was dancing up and down with delight. "Looks like it is play time again Joey! Get back to you in a minute girl." He went about getting nude, hung his clothing, and was soon right back at my bottom, rubbing Chubby up and down between my buns in the warm drippy clef. "Ready or not baby, daddy is back to make another baby for you!" The drum pounded in my ears, taking a very long time to bring us to the final climatic drum roll. I loved it, tossing my head from side to side as I pounded against the door with his every thrust, leaving another slick down the door to dry. "I'd have you clean this door with your tongue girl if I didn't think it could be loaded with paint lead in this old apartment building. I would not want my baby to get led poisoning." He turned me facing out on the peg. He switched on the TV and crawled on the bed watching, every once in awhile looking over to me and smiling.

Before too long he turned off the TV, lifted me off the peg down firmly on to my feet, wiped my ass well with the towel and ushered me into the bathroom. He told me to clean up well, shower and come back to bed for the night. He handed me a bottle of Fleet Enema and left. During the night, he was all over me, rubbing, sucking and taking his pleasures. He had not showered, so I had his scent all over me when the alarm went off at 5am. Before I left, he handed me a bag full of prophylactics in assorted sizes and reminded me to always use them since I had become so sexually active these last few weeks. He gave me another lecture on the importance of practicing safe sex with all my sex partners and sent me home before grandma awoke.

At 10:30am I was standing out on the sidewalk when Blake pulled up and motioned me into the van. Handsome as ever, dressed in his Storm Trooper Uniform, I bounced into the passenger seat, gave him a, "Good Morning Blake!" He took my hand, put it on his crotch, held it there and said, "Ready for some more of this baby?" I squeezed him and answered, "With this little softie?" He responded, "Oh, she has a smart mouth this morning," as he headed the van down the street. I asked, "Where does someone like you live Blake?" He answered, "You're about to find out today Joey. Buckle up baby!" It was not too long and Blake was driving through South San Francisco and into a section of Daily City where I had never been. He pulled up in front of a beautiful old Victorian property, freshly painted, looking grand. When he ushered me into the house, I couldn't believe how beautiful the place looked with all the stained glass windows and ornate moldings and woodwork. A big swastika was hanging on the wall along with pictures of Hitler, Mussolini, and even Castro. There were benches set up, indicating this was a meeting place for the Arian brotherhood organization - Flags, literature on a table, the works. He led me through that room toward the back and up a flight of stairs leading down a hallway. Doors were open along the route giving me a glimpse of a large dormitory with cots lined up for sleeping and a couple of bathrooms. He led me to a closed door at the end of the hallway. The minute I stepped through that door I realized I was in for another gang-bang session. About 12 Arian Brothers were standing there completely nude at parade rest. They automatically went to attention as Blake and I entered and gave the Nazi salute, even clicking their de-booted heals together. What a surprise!

I realized Blake had obviously planned this get together. He was definitely their leader, as he shouted something in German and they all went to parade rest again. He continued in English giving orders to the troops. I noticed that all of the guys had a swastika tattooed on their left arm just like Blake. Some had other similar tattoos all over their arms and torsos. Most of the guys were average endowed, a few like Blake, well above average. There were two that looked to be monsters, one a skinny guy with a groin full of bright red hair and the other guy looked to be a blond Swede or Norwegian. The blond guy reminded me of a horse with a long foreskin hanging down inches off the huge head. I just stared at his dick and he noticed my eyes checking him out, smiling and licking his lips at me as our eyes met. What really caught my attention were the four beautiful young men about my age, tied, gagged and suspended from the ceiling in leather harnesses. They each shaved of all body hair and had buzz cuts similar to mine. Butch and another stepped forward and undressed me as Blake announced, "This is Joey, our new bitch boys, a real hot number, likes blind meat, and rough anal sex among other things you will have to find out for yourselves. Hang her up with Jamie, Lenny, Jackie and Teddy. Remember troopers, "Safe Sex!" I was glad to hear those two words after what Trooper Jerry Gallagher had told me about the HIV AIDS virus last night. Blake spoke in German again giving his flock additional orders and I was led to the other four, tied, gagged, put in a harness and hoisted up with another block and tackle.

Blake shouted, "Dismissed," and the troopers headed for us. Hands were all over me feeling, rubbing, poking and tickling me. One guy lifted my legs up and hooked them into Velcro ties attached to the harness, leaving me in a precarious position with my bottom side ready for action. He fondled my ass, ran his hands up between my buns. When he realized I was wearing a butt plug, he poked it repeatedly until I was hard, excited and oozing pre-cum. He removed the plug and dropped it to the floor and his fingers went to work on me. His dick was hard, standing up almost touching his stomach as he loosened the knotted rope of the block and tackle and lowered me right over the lubricated prophylactic covering his manhood. Thank goodness I had lubed up well that morning and the guy was of average size or my ass would have been on fire. The guy started out slow, but before long, he was merciless with his thrusts once he found where my hot zone lay. He had me drooling with ecstasy when he shot his load. Another guy mounted me and continued the assault, as two other guys pinched my nipples and nibbled on me waiting their turn at my love canal. This guy was especially long, but relatively thin and plowed new territory without a problem. As I looked to my right, Jamie, Lenny, Jackie and Teddy were receiving about the same treatment as me. A few minutes later, I noticed that they had flipped the harness on both Lenny and Jamie so both their ass and face were accessible and being filled with man meat. Sure enough, another adjustment made. They flipped me too and came at me from both ends. Butch took my face in his hands and held the bottle of Amyl Nitrate to my nose! He quickly spread my lips open with his thumbs and in he went, balls slapping against my chin. He seemed large, quite large. After taking

Trooper Gallagher last night as I did, I was able to swallow his appendage as he worked it in and out over my throat muscles. I was slurping him down with each stroke as my ass pulsated for the guy in the rear. That guy up my behind was chewing and biting on the back of my legs and what he could reach of my thighs as he pounded his meat to me.

I fell into total submission as more amyl was put to my nose. This was really getting good as I felt the need to explode with all this stimulation from both ends building within. Another guy stepped up and started to nibble and bite on my inner thighs. That did it for me! I squirmed, I shuttered, and I squirted all over the floor. He grabbed under me and pinched my nipples repeatedly. This was wonderful, gloriously stimulating as the amyl kept me undulating over the thruster in my rear and Blake playing my pipes. I went out for a spell.

When I awoke to reality, the big Swede lined up at my bottom eating my pussy and sucking as if he had a mouth full of candy before him. He kept running his rough tongue up and down between my pinkie and my nuts, chewing on them, coming back down to push his tongue inside again. He took that little head-trip three times before he stepped up to me and started to push his monster into me. Blake gave me a big hit on the bottle and said, "That should do it for her Ludwig!" Well Ludwig pushed the head in and my insides convulsed from the amyl and sucked him right in until his balls were spread over my butt cheeks. I damn near shot my wad again from that one deep plunge. He began, slowly at first, sliding in and out of me, raking the massive head over my little walnut, as Blake kept putting the bottle to my nose. I was so turned on I just jumped, wiggled and squeezed on his meat with my muscles. I was in whore heaven enjoying the fruits of my current experiences.

I found myself begging, "Harder Ludwig! Please fuck me harder Ludwig! Oh YES! YES! YES! THAT'S THE WAY I LIKE IT! OH YEEEEAAAA!" My balls pulled up and delivered another huge fountain of spunk all over the floor. He just kept pumping as he leaned over and slurped, nibbled and sucked on my back between plunges. I knew it would not be long and he would be reaching his climax. Sure enough, my pulsating muscles took him right up to the top in two more thrusts. As he shot his load he shouted, "HOT FUCKING CUNT GIRL - WHEEEEE!" He lay over me exhausted, dripping his scent all over me. After all this activity with sweating men, I smelled like a happy whore. I loved it, inhaled the wonderful scent of spent men all over me.

Blake shouted, "Shower, clean up and dress guys, the girls are going to spend some special time now with their Owner Masters, the guy that brought them to share with you! Now, do you each see the benefits associated with bringing more young sweet lambs into our flock for pleasure men?" At that, he had us five lowered and each master stepped forward, lifted the other four cubs into their arms and carried off to what I assumed would be separate semi-private cubicles somewhere in this huge old house. I had noticed that Blake did not partake in the gang-bang, just walked around checking that everyone had taken care of their immediate sexual needs. Now that portion of the festivities ended, Blake walked over to Ludwig, said something to him. Ludwig came to me, lifted me into his arms and followed Blake down the hallway, down the stairs to the first floor. Blake held the door open to a large bedroom on the back corner of the building, as Ludwig entered and placed me in the center of a large king size bed covered with a clean sheet. He stood at the side of the bed and awaited instructions from Blake, as Blake took off his storm trooper uniform and hung it in a nearby closet. He pulled a few items from the closet and spoke to Ludwig on his way to the bathroom. "Keep Joey entertained Ludwig as usual, but don't cum again until I get back. Joey, I will be back in just a few minutes and join you both."

Ludwig took the opportunity to lick, suck, kiss and nibble all over me. He climbed up over my chest and choked me a few time trying to get his monster dick down my throat. Even soft, I couldn't even begin to get that monster down. It was just too big around, but it sure tasted and smelled great. I just nursed on it until I felt Blake's hands running up and down my inner thighs, one of my most sensitive body locations. I spread my legs wide, closed my eyes and felt his lips and tongue go up and down over my inner thighs. He said something in German to Ludwig and Ludwig rolled off me and plopped to my left side. When I opened my eyes Blake was on his knees between my spread legs looking down into my eyes. I must have looked surprised indeed! He was dressed in a black lace short Teddy, his hairy chest hair poking up from the lace bodice and from his armpits. Below he was wearing a pair of fancy lace panties that were open at the crotch for easy access, and his cock was jetting out. He made it bounce at me as he said. "Roll over on your stomach babe! Ludwig, you know where to go big guy!" My mind flashed, "What the fuck, is this guy a transvestite, a cross dresser, or just plain weird? I lay over on my stomach and Blake slipped his monster dick into me. He buried in me, his balls pressed against my buns.

Suddenly I felt more weight upon me, turned my head to one side and realized that Ludwig was leaned over Blake's back feeding his dick between the laced panties and right into his caboose. Blake let out a huge moan and shouted, "Fuck yes Ludwig! Fuck my hot ass trooper." Needless-to-say, even with both Blake and Ludwig supporting their weight off me, I was being pounded into the mattress as their lust took over their actions.

I shouted, "You two are suffocating me guys!" They rolled over on their sides in one move taking me with them and continued to lunge and pleasure themselves. Finally I could breathe and enjoy this three way union myself too. It didn't take long for me to ejaculate first, setting off Blake, in turn bringing Ludwig to climax. We fell asleep in that position for a while until I felt Blake pumping his ass back over Ludwig's monster and stick his dick into me again. This action very slowly continued until we all three dropped another load, mine going all over the sheet.

As Blake drove me home that afternoon, I asked him about what we did. He was not embarrassed to talk about it at all. He told me he liked it both ways, and liked to dress up in women's nightwear when he did. He liked the feel of silk and lace next to his skin. He told me he especially liked Ludwig's big dick in him. He admitted that he was bi, but only Ludwig was aware of that fact and fucked him frequently when he was feeling submissive or when they had three-ways together, so he could fuck a hot ass too. I was not quite sure if I wanted to do it again, but when I looked over at handsome Blake my ass twitched with excitement. He said, "Pick you up again at 10:30am next Wednesday Joey babe!" I went into the house that afternoon shaking my head, totally amazed at my experience today, especially after learning that macho Blake was bi, and liked to dress up in women's undergarments and have the big Swede Ludwig pound his ass with that big dick, obviously often, and keeping it private and secretive from his skinhead Arian brothers.

CHAPTER 9

After dinner, I thought a lot about what had transpired today with Blake, Ludwig, and their Arian Brotherhood today. Did I really want to be associated in any way with this bunch of skinhead Nazi Nuts? Well, I had a whole week to decide if I wanted to become a sex toy for the bunch of them just to be with Blake and now Ludwig. Seeing Blake in those lacy girlie teddy and panties kind of changed my impression of the handsome dude too, leaving a rather unattractive impression on my image of him as a 100% macho skinhead top. He had said, "Pick you up again at 10:30am next Wednesday Baby!" Would I be waiting for him next Wednesday or would I make myself scarce?

After dinner and cleanup, I used 'Old Red' for a quick douche, soaked in the tub and dressed. I kept checking the windows across the street for signs that Trooper Gallagher was home and wanting me again tonight. When I checked my emails, Master Jake had posted a reminder that tomorrow morning I should be at his house at 9am so he and the Major could start with my dungeon training. I send him a reply confirming, as instructed and read a couple of updates to stories

I had been reading on Nifty again. It was well after 11:30pm when I last looked across the street for signs of life. Since there were none, I started to undress when the doorbell rang. I knew grandma would be sound asleep and never hear it, so trotted downstairs to answer the door to see who could possibly be ringing our doorbell at this late hour. I opened the front door and stepped on to the bricked area between the door and the security gate. Ludwig the big Swede was standing there in the fog and cold with a big smile on his face.

"Hi Joey, I come in yes?"

"Damn Ludwig it is going on to midnight. What are you doing here at this hour?"

He answered, "I really need you tonight Joey, I so horny I want to bust britches!" This pissed me off a bit. Here he was standing just outside my security gate in just a tee shirt, his uniform britches and his black storm trooper boots in the blistering cold fog wanting to get serviced, not even knowing who lives in the house with me. This well confirmed my suspicions from earlier in the day. Ludwig was not overly bright, maybe a few cards short of a full deck plus he spoke such broken English it was a bit difficult to communicate with the big Swede. He continued looking sad and alone like a big lost teddy bear. "Please Joey, Everyone gone. I'm all alone and really need to make sex. See how I make big tent and drip in britches!" He immediately pulled his monster dick out and poked it through bars of the security gate. It was big alright and it was certainly dripping cock-snot big time like a dripping faucet. I was flabbergasted at his boldness, but I cannot say it did not take my breath away at the same time. I couldn't take my eyes off the huge blind meat as it hung between the bars, pulsating and dripping cock nectar on to the breezeway's red tiled floor.

I did some quick thinking! I knew it was going to be impossible to get him to leave. Hard telling how he would respond to a straight out refusal to take care of his sexual needs. He could awaken the entire neighborhood with a display of sexual driven furry, but there was no way I could bring him into the house. He would be back every night if I allowed him in just once. However, I could not keep my eyes off his monster dick. It was huge and beckoned me to it like a honing beacon. It naturally flustered me as it dribbled before my very eyes.

"Ludwig, how did you get here and who knows you have come to see me big guy?" He answered, "I come in Blake's van, parked down street, all parking full near house! Blake is in San Jose for the night with Butch and Troy. No be back until tomorrow. I horny now Joey! Yes, I come in and spend the night with you, fuck you good girl – make you feel good - you like?" I said.

"Ludwig, put your dick back in you pants, pointing to his rod. Wait here, let me get my cap and coat and I will go for a ride with you. We can do it in the back of the van, but you can not come in the house." He gave me a big smile and said, "OK Joey, I do what you say so I can fuck you tonight!" I had been watching the windows in Jerry's apartment. They were still dark. I guessed he had the night shift tonight. I made sure my coat had a few large rubbers and plenty of KY in the pocket and returned. He put his arm around my waist and walked me along in the cold fog to the van squeezing my ass. I figured I would service him orally in the back of the van and get him headed home quickly without any problems.

He opened the side door of the van and I noticed that the mattress was still down, but it was cold. He started the engine and soon it started to warm up inside. He said, "Joey, I like you, same as Blake, maybe more - you're so pretty and smell so good" He was already taking off his clothing!

"Ludwig, pull all the curtains shut and flip on these two little lights on each side so we can see in here!" I knew I was going to have to direct him or I would find myself bounced around in the dark getting stuck with his monster poker and end up black and blue. I had not started to disrobe yet, figuring if I could blow him, get this big guy off and be gone quickly. He was so intent on getting nude, he did not realize I was just watching him, had not started to take my clothing off yet. The minute he was nude, I pulled my cap, shoved it in my pocket, dove into his groin and sucked him up. I teased his balls with one hand as I rolled my tongue up into the foreskin and around the head until he just lay back and let me have my way with him. I brought him to a quick huge climax. He lifted my head up to his lips and kissed me. I could see his dick was still hard and twitching.

"Now I make love with you Joey and make you feel good too - OK! You take off all clothes now too! I want you nude like today again - YES!"

I said, "No Ludwig, that's all tonight Big Guy - maybe another time!" That was the wrong thing to say! He grabbed me, pulled me to him and started nearly ripping the clothing off me until he had me nude. Here, I thought I could control him as Blake did with orders and commands. Well was I wrong! He knew what he wanted and there was no way he was not going to get it all, everything he wanted. When I was completely nude, he laid me on my back on the mattress and virtually licked and sucked, slurping his saliva all over me. He took special interest on my inner thighs and anus once he had my legs up in the air over his shoulders. His tongue was a machine, well oiled and trained to please! Never, until now, has anyone ever tongued me for as long as he did. Blake had him trained well in preparing his bitch for a hot ride with fantastic foreplay. He had me pushing back against him and moaning, lusting for this pleasure. I finally could resist him no more, wanted it possibly even more than he did.

My hand reached my coat at the side, pulled out the KY and a large rubber and handed it to him. I said, "OK Ludwig, grease me, put on the rubber and do your thing big guy!" He knew the routine! Greased middle finger, then fingers added as he opened me up, roll of the rubber over his massive joystick and soon I felt the massive head pushing against my pink rosebud. Plop the massive head put fire in the hole. He knew to wait a moment, let me relax before he pushed in further. He looked down into my eyes, showed his teeth in a big smile.

He whispered, "Big dick burn now yes - soon feel good and make you smile big like Ludwig! You very tight Joey - feel real good!" He did not wait long before he was pushing in further. When the monster pressed against my walnut, I began to relax and feel full but good! He sensed my ass muscles relaxing and rotated on that spot until I let out a low moan.

"Mmmm! Oh yes, right there - that is the spot!" He massaged that spot until I came alive inside, sending waves of pleasure through me. In one thrust, he buried his dick and his balls pressed against my bottom. He knew he possessed me from that moment forward.

"You like now Joey - I fuck you good - make you smile and coo like little baby!" His head dropped to my chest and he slurped and nibbled on my nipples as he turned loose on my anal canal. You talk about a stallion in action. He was rutting me, and yes, he had me smiling, moaning and cooing just like he said. This big guy was a fuck machine and had enough energy to propel me to the outer limits into infinity. I just held on tight, delighting in his assault on my tight pussy canal and over my rock hard walnut. As much as I tried to prolong this great feeling, he had me spraying in record time. My pulsating anal muscles took him over the top, causing him to shudder, stiffen and drop a second load. His grunting noises filled my ears as the sound of a wild animal. He hesitated for a minute and then continued to rut and long dick me with that heavenly Swedish hot rod. My mind was wondering, totally engrossed in the pleasure he was giving me. He looked down into my dreamy eyes and said, "You squeeze now Joey, I make baby again for you." He opened full throttle again, grunting and groaning animal sounds, plunging, thrusting, and rotating his groin into me. I was wild and almost shouting his name when he finally brought us to another wild climax.

The van had become very hot and he was sweating, dripping his scent all over me. He dropped my legs off his shoulders and pulled from me. He crawled to the front and shut off the engine, returned to my side and ran a towel over us cleaning up the mess I had left on us both. He disposed of the full rubber and put on a fresh one. He grabbed a big old blanket, turned off the lights, crawled in behind me and covered us both and slipped back into me. I felt so satisfied, so complete in his arms, his aroma filling my head. He was obviously use to sleeping regularly with someone, he went right to sleep. The last thing I remember as my ass muscles twitched over his semi-flaccid cock was his nibbling on my neck, shoulder and ear. We must have slept for quite awhile before I awoke. His dick was coming alive in me again, lengthening, expanding and slightly pulsating. He seemed still asleep, steady breath against my neck. I just squeezed and massaged the hardness, feeling it pulsate each time I gave it a gentle squeeze. It was wonderful. I was so comfortable and cozy, his warmth radiating against me. I could have laid there and continued this forever, happily filled with emotion and enjoying him expanding and filling me, spreading me inside. He muttered Swedish or German and drooled on my neck, still half asleep. All I could understand was the name Blake, which confirmed my suspicion that he slept and fucked Blake. No wonder he had turned Blake into such a bottom the way he used that big Swedish dick on a hot pussy. I gave him a couple of hard squeezes with my anus muscles and he came awake and plowed me again to a successful explosion for both of us. Ludwig had mastered the art of foreplay and used that big monster dick of his to turn a bottom into a total submissive. He was a man beast alright – all man to the core!

I put my digital wristwatch to my eyes, pushed the button to activate the small light and it read 4:35am. I knew I had to get dressed and be on my way soon. I started to pull from him, but he held me to him and whispered, "Joey, where you go?"

"It's time for me to go Big Guy! Next time call me first OK, Blake has my telephone number. No more surprise visits!" I leaned over, gave him a kiss and headed back home. As I entered the house, tiptoed up to my bedroom, and undressed to head to the bathroom for a good clean-out and hot bath, my mind was still in the back of that van with Ludwig. I reevaluated Ludwig's intelligence, and realized I may have been too critical in thinking he was retarded. Maybe he just seemed retarded because he had not learned the English language enough yet to communicate properly. Hell, someone as wonderful in bed as he was did not have to talk at all. His dick communicated just fine! Then my mind went to thinking about what today's activities with Master Jake and the Major would entail. I hummed a little tune as I soaked in the tub just a bit concerned about going back into that dungeon this morning.

Along about 9:10am I headed out for Master Jake's house. I gave a buzz at the front door and his voice roared back at me, "That you Joey?"

"Yes Master Jake Sir!" The door clicked and I went in and undressed, folding my clothing and putting them in the foyer closet. Since I had already, cleaned and bathed, I headed right to the exercise room and started my routines on the Bow-Flex machine. I was just about finished with my final set and both Master Jake and the Major entered the room dressed in sexy leather harnesses, boots, and leather riding chaps with removable crotch inserts. Talk about breathtaking! I jumped to my feet at Attention, or was it Display Attention and saluted the two handsome officers. The Major said, "At Ease Grunt," turned to the Colonel and said, "The Boys looking fine today now that he got rid of all that long hair - real fine!"

The Colonel got a funny look on his face and said. "Did I tell you to cut off your hair boy? I wanted to do that today. What the hell, it looks great, but still worth four good lashes with the strap for doing it without my approval. Major, give him four good ones when you get him strung up this morning!" The Major got a smirk on his face looking directly into my eyes. Damn that dude was handsome - my cock started to rise just looking at the two of them standing there together in their leather.

While I was still at parade rest, cock rising, the Major stepped up to me, cupped my balls in his hand and squeezed my package until he obviously meant it to hurt. Tears came to my eyes and my dick went limp. He grasped my flaccid member and led me all the way down into the bowels of the dungeon. The damn place was as scary and depressing as ever to me. It gave me the shivers - still cold, dark and reeked of death. I noticed Master Jake had not accompanied us. I became even more scared and wrapped my arms around the Major in a death grip. He pushed me away and said, "Straighten up boy! I'm going to make a man out of you in this place; so get use to the place.

You will be spending a lot of time down here and similar places in the future!"

I asked, "Sir, please Sir, can you open your cock flap and let your cock and balls out where I can see them? You are such a handsome devil and I kind of forgot what your cock looked like Sir it may help in taking my mind off this dark creepy place!"

He smiled and answered, "Not till after the discipline the Colonel ordered boy. Now get your butt up on the horse and lay over it, face down. All I want to see is your ass in the air." I hopped up on the leather horse as he said, exposing my ass to him. He stepped to the cabinet and returned with the strap, displaying it to me. He stepped behind me so I could not see him. The leather horse and mount hid my view of him. "Now count them out boy, and then say 'Thank you Sir, may I have another?' If you don't count them out, we start all over Grunt!" I felt his hand rubbing my ass and between the cheeks. Whack, came the first blow! It put tears to my eyes and I failed to give my response I was so stuck with pain and shock. "Bad! Bad! You did not respond boy, so we start all over!" Whack! I jumped but responded immediately this time.

"One - thank you Sir may I have another?" He rubbed my ass again and I waited for the next, not knowing when it would come. Whack! I let out a scream but responded, "Two - thank you Sir - may I have another?" The next one came immediately. Whack! I was in real pain, a cramp had started in my leg, but I responded. "Three - thank you Sir - may I have another!" He rubbed my ass with the palm of his hand and down the leg I was twitching. Suddenly I felt the final Whack! The blood seemed to have rushed to my head almost putting me out. The cramp in my leg was major! I shouted, "Four - thank you Sir - may I have another?" He said, "No that is all for now Grunt." He helped me to my feet so I could work out the cramp. He said, "Now next time you ask the Colonel before you do anything drastic to your body or hair boy! Let this be a lesson to you that he is the Master and you are his lowly Cub Grunt!"

"The Colonel and I had a long talk about your progress to date. He told me that you are already quite submissive, tolerate a great deal of pain for a beginner, do a fair job giving oral sex, quite accomplished and crave anal sex. He said you have a tendency to ejaculate prematurely and without permission. We term that kind of young man an 'Unbridled Rapid Shooter.' We can not have you shooting off any time you want now can we - gets things all messy and sticky when we play with you! A Master always takes his pleasures, which vary from master to master. Some are totally dominant, love to humiliate, swear and cuss and administer pain. Others are dominant, but like to play the submissive roll, become bottoms when having sex – they are a rare breed indeed. The General is like that - dominant because of his position of authority, but likes to take the submissive roll during sex. Get the picture! If you pleasure any master with his needs, deliver what he wants of you, then he rewards you with the pleasures you like. In your case, most likely, anal sex, but that could change as you learn new things. You will soon learn my pleasures as your trainer boy. When I get through with you, my pleasures will be your pleasures and you will learn to crave them as your own. However, remember - you go over the top and skeet without permission and your punishment will be severe with that Cat-of-nine-tails you got a taste of from your Master already. You understand?"

All I could say was, "Sir, yes Sir!"

"Let's get started then. I am going to give you a stop word and a slow down word. A stop word is a word you say to your master when you cannot take any more of what he is doing to you. A slow down word is for him to slow, continue at a slower pace until you get use to what he is doing. Do you understand?"

"Sir, yes Sir," was all I need say, but the wheels in my head were spinning all kinds of weird scenarios, wondering just how kinky these guys played with their Grunt Cubs."

He continued, "Your slow down word will be YELLOW, your stop word will be RED! Just remember - you say the word RED, I stop what I am doing to you and you forfeit your pleasures for the day. No cock for you that day! Do you have any questions?" I asked, "Sir, Major Sir, what do I call you, I don't even know your first name Sir?" He answered, "Sir, or Major Sir, either is acceptable! You do not need to know my name yet boy until I know you are trainable and closed mouthed!" He turned me sideways and gave me a good hard pop with his palm across my sore, red buns causing me to let out a loud squeal.

He stood erect, hands on hips, and any kind look he may have had faded from his face. "Now get your ass down on your knees, get that pretty face of yours in the air and squeal like a piglet, then give my boots a spit shine you little squealer." I dropped to my knees, looked up into his eyes and squealed twice. He sneered down at me and I went about cleaning his boots as ordered. He kept moving the boot making it difficult to clean. He kept lifting and rubbing the boot over my face until I was finally able to complete the spit shine. "Squeal again and then shine the other boot piglet!" I could see the Major had a thing for humiliation. When I figured the second boot was clean, I looked up at him and smiled. He demanded, "What the fuck you smiling at bitch?"

I answered, "Your personality change Sir! How dominant you have become in just a flash of time! I like it Sir! Talk dirty to me Sir!" He got red in the face, probably thinking I was mocking him.

"Just shut the fuck up boy, not another peep out of you! Now get your hot buns up here and bite on my nipples." I jumped to my feet and admired his nipples for just a fleeting moment before I started executing his order. His nipples were huge with big round areolas surrounding them. "I said, bite my nipples Boy! When I tell you to do something, do not hesitate, just do it boy!" He grabbed my head between his huge hands and pushed my lips to his left nipple. "NOW LICK, CHEW, AND BITE IT BOY! I LIKE IT ROUGH SO HANG ON IT BOY!" I gave him exactly what he wanted! Almost immediately, it delivered a bit of clear fluid with little taste, possibly slightly of no fat milk. When I switched to the other nipple, it did the same. The harder I nipped, sucked and bit, the better he liked it. He smelled very masculine as I performed my services on his nipples.

He was rubbing his crotch against me and moaning when he suddenly pulled away and ordered. "Open up my cock piece and lift my cock and balls out, get on your knees and put your face to my family jewels and inhale the smell so you know me well boy." I opened the flap, lifted his package out, and instantly went to my knees between his spread legs, face rubbing against his crotch inhaling his masculinity. The smell of leather and beast was overwhelming. "Make love to them with your eyes and rub your face on it, but do not put your lips or tongue on them. Learn the feel of them against your skin - lift them in your hands and inspect them - worship them with your eyes boy and rub your pretty face all over it!" I spent some time admiring, fondling and checking every inch of his huge 10inch uncircumcised dick and huge balls. I noticed he had a big vein spiraling down the shaft and a small mole near the base on the underside. "Pull the foreskin back and sniff around the head now boy and tell me what you see and what you like about my package."

"Oh Sir, I don't know where to begin! I love the masculine scent, this big vein running down here around the shaft, even this little mole hidden on the underside. I love your long loose foreskin, the way it slides on and off over your big mushroom shaped cockhead and glands. I especially like your size and big dangling balls Sir. "Oh Sir, you have me so turned on, can I lick and suck on it?"

He gave me an immediate answer. "No boy, you get the prize as your reward after you make me happy and do everything I want you to do for me without hesitation and without having any accidental premature ejaculations along the way. You have to earn your rewards boy! I will be taking my pleasures with your body and teaching you to enjoy and crave what I like to do with pretty, young Cub Boys! Get up on your feet now boy!" He led me to the cabinet and loaded my arms with items he pulled off the shelves and pegs. "To the table and spread them out." He put a harness on me, hooked it up to D rings to the two cables and hoisted me up until my feet barely touched the floor. He put wrist cuffs and ankle cuffs on me, hooked my wrists behind my back to the harness. He took a long rod and hooked it to my ankle cuffs, which spread my feet about a full yard and held them in place. He stood behind me, pulled my butt plug out, replaced it with a curved dildo and pushed it up against my prostrate gland. It made me ooze pre-cum and start to get hard again. He hooked it to the electric cord from under the table, put the metal clamps on my nipples, the metal cock ring ball spreader/stretcher and cinched them up until I found it quite uncomfortable. He attached the electric cords to each item, stuck a huge ball gag into my mouth and fastened the leather belt around behind my head. He pushed earplugs into my ears, then pulled this huge, black leather, head mask over my head and bound it securely. This left me deaf, dumb and blind, suspended and totally helpless with my legs spread hooked up to electric cords at three of my erogenous zones. I felt his hands running up and down over my body, playing with my cock until I was hard and oozing pre-cum again. He turned on the electricity to the dildo and I was feeling very good.

Suddenly he activated the electronic stimulator and my body convulsed, just as I experience when Master Jake had me hooked up. He left me hanging, the intermittent shocks making me go limp, but the dildo bringing me right back and excited again and again. Once in awhile I could feel him pulling on my cock and balls or rubbing his hands over me. To add more stimulation, he began to bite and chew on my ass cheeks, then licked, sucked and nibbled up and down over my inner thighs,, one of my most erogenous zones I would almost SHOOT my load, but knew I must not or get a good taste of the Cat-of-nine-tails, which I had laid on the table.

The pain intensified as he obviously turned up the electric shocks. I started to hum, hum the pain away, hoping it would all stop as it did before with Master Jake. It took longer, but eventually each time my body convulsed I felt a warm pleasure creep through me from the source of each shock. I hummed my heart away in total ecstasy as he kept increasing the electric current. I was so turned on I wanted to SKEET and blow my cum for 10 feet, but my mind kept going to that

Cat and the horrible experience I had when it was put to me before. I suddenly felt four hands rubbing and playing with my body, stroking my cock between shocks. Eventually I just passed out and hung limp. When I awoke the electric stimulation was over, gone, complete, and I wanted to scream for it to return. The devices were removed quickly, including the head mask, ear plugs and ball gag.

When my eyes adjusted to the light, Master Jake and the Major were looking at me in astonishment. Master Jake spoke first, "You did well Joey, you never cease to amaze me boy! Your tolerance to pain is unbelievable; you just go into the alpha state and hum it all away. Only one other boy in Vietnam I trained had your tolerance for pain boy. That was many years ago, before you were born. I'm proud of you boy!" The Major said, "You are my first you little pain slut. I guess you earned your pleasures." He lowered the hoist and my master fed his dick to me as the Major greased up and gave me the meat from the rear. I moaned and when the Master's cock slipped into my mouth I felt wanted, needed, and loved by both these beautiful men. They took their time making sure I enjoyed each and every plunge until I was shaking with lust and pleasure. The Major exploded first shouting, "SHOOT BOY - SKEET!" It sent me into one explosion after the other as the Master filled my throat with his seed. They released me from my bindings and the three of us showered together in the big open shower in the dungeon before going upstairs.

The Master told me to dress and be back at 10am in the morning for another training session. I was still so horny I walked all the way home with the butt plug keeping me so hard I had to keep my hand in my pocket to keep from tenting my baggies. I wanted more, lots more of their games taught to me. I was a slut and did not care who knew it. What could I do with the rest of my day to get some more pleasure from a man? It was only noon! As I started to enter the security gate at home, Trooper Jerry Gallagher shouted for me to come over from the window in his apartment. He buzzed me in and I was in his apartment taking my clothing off in minutes. I virtually threw myself into his arms and begged him to fuck me. He lit right up as a trooper should at the sound of pussy! It must have been his day off, as I did not have many cloths to take off him to get to his big dick, but he made me beg for it at least five times before he delivered. He finally put the cuffs on me, hooked me on the door peg, and put the meat to me. He humped my ass twice before he lowered me off the peg and made me clean up all my messes off the closet door with a bottle of Windex and a towel. He had me clean him with my lips and tongue and I just held on to him and inhaled his male scent.

He said, "You're a little bitch in heat today Joey! Stick around and I will fuck you again in awhile baby!" In the meantime how about I get a few pictures of that new haircut, a couple of that hot bare ass of yours, and a couple of your cock, balls and that little patch of blond hair for my scrapbook." He led me to the living room and I posed for him, bending over showing my pinkie, my cock and balls, all without a view of my face. We viewed and printed them out on glossy paper, laughing, horse playing with each other, as the printer ground out the prints. My trooper was a real joy to be around when he was in a playful mood. He liked to hug, kiss, fondle and tickle me. I ate it up, kept coming back for more trying to outdo him with my displays of lust for him. His armpits became my favorite rest area. Once I was in that moist hairy cavern I turned into a sweat slut and he just gave into me, carried me to the sofa and let me eat him all over. I loved the big guy and he knew it! He was extra special in my book – my Italian Stallion.

CHAPTER 10

Between noon and 4:30pm Thursday afternoon Trooper Jerry Gallagher and I made love four times, two with me hanging off the closet peg, him rubbing his sweating body up and down my backside. Then one, me laid over the back of the sofa with my ass in the air and he rutting me making wild animal sounds. The final poke was sitting on his lap facing him in his computer chair so he could suck on my nipples as I played ride the pony, stallion in his case. He let me lick and suck on his lips, face, neck and ears as I slowly massaged his stallion lodged up my Wazoo. I made it last, having total control over this mating. We became as one - lips, tongues probing and searching for the ultimate passage to satisfy our passions. He was equally as horny today as I. His nips and bites over my neck and shoulders were serious business. He liked to mark his territory like all male animals. I finally asked him if he could refrain from marking me so severely, especially on the neck where they showed so prominently. His answer was, "You're a little bitch in heat and I just go crazy in your arms Joey! Sorry, I'll put them all down lower from now on, right on your' hot little ass. How's that!" He laughed and gave me another round of playing grab ass. The guy was phenomenal, like a big brother after sex. How could I not love him?

"It is 4:30pm Joey, you best get home for dinner with Grandma Schmidt." I shuffled on home still horny, my butt plug reminding me of that fact. After dinner and a clean out, hot bath, I started reliving the events of the day. I lay on the bed nude, my mind floated back to the anal, and electric shock the Major gave me and became so horny. I must have gone into that alpha state they talked about in the dungeon today, because I was feeling the same pleasures I felt earlier that morning. I think I fell asleep and it was all a dream, but knew I had to have a dick in me again tonight when

I awoke. I was lusting, literally lusting for an anal probing. I looked across the street and Trooper Jerry's windows were all in darkness. I rang the number Amos had given me and there was no answer. I even rang Daily City to the number Blake had given me. An answering machine answered, so I hung up, wondering where I could go to get what I needed. I even called Master Jake's house and there was no answer. Here I was, lusting for a man, any man to turn animal, probe and dominate me. What had those electrical stimuli done to me to make me so horny yet after having sexual release as many times as I did already today? All I knew, I had to have more or I would be up all night pacing the floor. The fog had not rolled in tonight as it had been doing for weeks now. I had learned by searching the Internet that both the Castro District and Polk Street were popular places with the gay crowd. Since Poke Street was much closer than the Castro was, I decided to catch the bus on Lombard, go the 20 or so blocks over to Polk, and see what mischief I could get into. I jumped off the bus at Van Ness and Broadway and walked down the one block to Polk. Polk Street was busy with guys, some walking hand in hand, others just doing as I. Sidewalk cafes were bustling with activity, as were the sidewalks - hot guys, old, young, and some teenagers like me. When I reached California Street, I noticed a bunch of what had to be hustlers, stepping up to cars, talking with the drivers, then either getting into the car or stepping back up on the curb and waving them on. I watched for awhile and saw some very nice cars with some hot drivers making the circle repeatedly looking at the meat rack of young boys displaying their young bodies to the clientele.

I turned on just watching the activity, their antics to bring attention to themselves. I decided to go closer, join them to see if any would talk to me. One of the hustlers, actually the best looking one in the group walked up to me and said. "Hey! New kid on the block, huh - my names Duke - what's yours'?" I answered, "Joey." He was dressed in a pair of frayed, worn, faded denim wranglers. His knees exposed where the material had split from wear. They fit him like a glove, especially over his groin. His dick lay down his left thigh, clearly outlined in the faded denim. He had on a tight white tee shirt that displayed two nice nipples and his nice lean body to a tee. He reminded me of John Travolta when he played in 'Grease.' He put his arm around my waist and led me to one side. Get rid of the wool cap and coat boy and you will have better luck at this business; they like to get a good look at your face and body, especially the body. You're new at this ain't you kid?" I answered, "Yea, my first trip down here!" He looked me over, top to bottom, pushed my cap into my coat pocket, tied the coat around my neck by the sleeves, stepped back and looked me over for another moment. He pulled my Baggies down until they were barely hanging off my cock which really made me tent. I was so excited just looking at this handsome creature. He groped me to feel my size, pulled my tight jersey loose in a couple of places and said, "That should do it boy - very sexy indeed! Get yourself some boots when you can boy!" I asked, "How much money do you earn and what do you say to these guys that pull up and wave you over?" He answered, "Hey, it depends on what kind of car they drive, whether I like their looks, and how broke I am! When I am flush, I'm expensive; when I'm hungry, I'm cheap. If they want me all night, I have gotten as much as $300 bucks. By the looks of you boy, pretty blond doll, as you are, you should be able to get big bucks. Just be careful, always ask them if they are cops and make them quote you a price for exactly what services they want. I have been doing this for a couple of years, make good money too. We hustlers stake our territory, and unless you play your cards right, you will have trouble working on this corner. Tell you what though! I'll take you under my wing tonight on a 70/30 basis, teach you the ropes if you want Joey boy. I have a lot of guys that come by looking for me – return customers that will pay good money to get into your pants. Stick with me and I'll make you some money. We got a deal?" I responded, "Hell, why not, 70/30 sounds a bit steep, how about 60/40?" Sure buddy, you are definitely hot and these John's will pay good money for you!"

"Now stick close to me, let me do the talking, just look young, pretty, don't smile, and don't say a word, just learn from the master. See that black Jaguar pulling down California. Return business - big bucks, nice pad, booze, drugs, into leather, no hassles, pay big bucks – two middle-aged guys that own a gay bar downtown south of Market and live in upper floors above the bar. They come by often late at night like this, one looking for dick, the other one looking for some pussy. Are you a top, a bottom or versatile, Joey. "I answered "Mostly Bottom I guess!" He smiled, "I should have guessed that, as pretty as you are Joey. I would fuck you in a second myself, free! As for me, never had a dick up my ass and never will either - macho man!" Hope you have a pocket full of lube and rubbers. I hope you like big dicks, Joey, as this one has a horse dick on him." I answered, "I do Duke, the bigger the better!" He said, "Good, he will open you up! He is pulling over Joey, just follow me and stay cool, emotionless, no smiles!" He patted me on my ass and stepped to the curb as the Jaguar stopped at the curb and the tinted window rolled down on the passenger's side. Duke said, "Howdy Dick! Mike still working the bar yet huh! Out looking for some boy pussy, look no further. Joey here is a rare find, handles big dicks well, but he is very expensive!" I could not hear the response, but the door opened and Duke told me to get in the front seat, as he got in forcing me to the middle. Dick's hand went immediately to my inner thigh and moved up until it was fondling my basket to see if the tent in my britches was real. "What a looker Duke, where you find this blond beauty," as he looked down into my baby blues? "It must be my lucky night running into you for Mike, but especially finding this little toe-headed beauty for me to ravish!"

Dick was a big burly bear man - full salt and pepper beard and a long ponytail, looked like a mountain man. He was not really what

I would describe as handsome, but he had a big smile that showed his pearly whites. His eyes and big full lips were his best features, eyes the lightest gray I have ever seen. They drew me right to him and held my attention. "What's you name beautiful?" I answered, "Joey!" He continued, "Well Joey, how about you fish me out and give me a squeeze or two while I drive us home and negotiate a price for you two to stay all night with your manager Duke here! Hope you are as smooth all over as your age indicates! You look to be one hot fuck boy!" By then I had his zipper down in his leather pants and was pulling his dick out. I said, "My god Dick, your mother named you right; you have a monster on you, a real fatty too!" I turned to Duke and said, "Be sure and charge him by the square inch!" It started to expand and harden as I fondled him. The thing must have been at least 13 or 14inches long, uncircumcised, and as big around as a beer can. I could not believe the feel of it, soft as silk! He looked at my expression and said, "So, you like the big stuff Joey?" I answered, "Yes, but I'm not sure about fighting with this monster - looks to be a killer whale!" He just chucked at my remark, and then said. "Well Joey, I'll get it into you boy - you can bet on it!" He pulled into the alley alongside the bar in the Mission District downtown and parked. Like all huge dicks, his too was pliable, soft to the touch. I folded it, pushed it back into his britches, and zipped up his leather pants. I stroked it under the leather a couple of times and was amazed that it reached a third of the way to his knee. There were about 10 Harley-Davidson bikes parked in the lot and five trucks, so I assumed it was a leather bar.

"Are you old enough to go into a bar boy?" I answered, "Eighteen Sir!" He continued, "What the hell, it is Thursday night, slow night, no cops around." He led Duke and me through the front door and there were about 15 guys in the bar, mostly drinking beer, playing pool, all dressed in tee shirts, denim or leather. All heads pointed toward us as we entered, eyes looking over both Duke and me. A tall slender guy about the same age as Dick, about 45, was behind the bar. He was very good looking, and wore a black leather vest and faded wranglers. He had a shaved head and a full, thick blond mustache, piercing green eyes. Dick ushered us over to him and said, "This is Mike, my business, domestic partner and better half Joey!

Mike, give us each a beer." Mike answered, "The kid 21, he looks to be about 16?" Duke responded right back, "Give the kid a beer Mike, he will need it when your old man sticks that dick of his in him." Mike smiled, brought the three of us a draft!" He undressed me with his eyes and said, "What a fucking beauty - where did you find this one Duke and does he know how to spread those legs of his wide enough for Big Daddy Dick's dick?" Mike had quick answers, "Why sure he does Mike, I trained him myself with this 10incher you like so well! He ain't cheap! He will cost you some big bucks, like $400 for the night. You know my price. Talk it over with Dick and bring us both another beer and a couple of those Ecstasy pills you have hidden away for special occasions like this so I can plug you good tonight."

He came back with the drafts and the pills, tried to negotiate a price of $300, but Mike held out for the full $400 saying, "Hell Mike, write it off as a necessary business expense you old moneybags. He's a lot cheaper than that fancy new Jaguar sedan, that new dually crew-cab Dodge pickup or those two Harley-Davidson bikes. Mike stopped him, "OK Duke, Mike really wants the kid, $400 for him, your usual $250, OK!" Mike went to the register, pulled out $650 and handed it to Duke. Duke counted out $160, stuffed it in my baggies and shoved the rest in his pocket. He looked at me and said, "Not too bad for one nights work huh kid! Stick with me and I'll make you a rich bitch!" I gave him a look to kill and said, "Sure, $490 for you and $160 for me, swell deal for you maybe!" He answered, "Well, what would you have earned without me tonight baby - nada most likely! RIGHT! I know the ropes and can get you the good customers Joey; so do not get greedy until you can pull in the cash all by yourself kid. Now take this damn pill, drink your beer and shut the fuck up and go sit with Dick like a good boy!" He shoved the pill in my mouth, put the other in his mouth, handed me the draft and said, "Down the hatch Joey - make a real slut out of you tonight and me into a wild stallion. One more thing Joey, these guys don't like to use rubbers, they sleep around a lot, so make sure you get a rubber on his dick before he screws you boy! I know you must still live at home boy! What time you have to be home in the morning?" I answered, "Before 5am 5:30am at the latest Duke!" He said, "Give me you ID Joey!"

He looked at it and said, "Eighteen alright, Joey Schmidt, blue eyes, blond hair, 3747 Scott Street - that's in the Marina District isn't it Joey?" I nodded my head yes, he handed it back to me and said, "OK, now get your ass over and sit next to Dick and do whatever he wants or I will take it out on your hide later!"

I sat next to Dick and he removed my coat from my neck and handed it to Mike to hang up on a peg on the wall. He ran his hands over my neck, shoulders and down my back and addressed Mike. "Ain't he a jewel babe, just look at this blond hair and his blue eyes? Just as you were about 25 years ago when I first met you! What a beauty, reminds me of you Mikie!" Dick led me around introducing me to all the guys in the bar. Each of them took the opportunity to probe and rub their hands over me, especially my hair and buns. A few of them actually rubbed their merchandise up and down over the cheeks of my ass. Biker hunks, smelling of man beast and leather, construction workers and longshoremen still in their grubby work clothes – torn and soiled tee shirts or plaid shirts open down the front displaying their muscled chests and tattoos. After one more draft, I began to warm all over. The warmth spread through my body quickly making me fidget. My dick got hard and my ass pulsated quickly! I stood in front of Dick and backed up until his dick rubbed on my ass and stood there with his warmth radiating against me. I found myself lusting for what I felt growing against my buns. He let out a chuckle and said, "Is my baby getting a bit horny or is it just my imagination?" I just moaned and put my hands behind me to feel that huge salami, rubbing my finger tips up and down over the shaft I felt laying down his thigh under leather. I could not control myself. I turned to him and asked. "Will you please make love to me Sir? I'm so horny for your big dick!" He answered, "Control yourself boy, we are open until 2am and it is only a little after midnight!" He popped me on the ass and lifted me on to a stool.

"I'm going to the bathroom Sir; I have to pee like a race horse!" He said, "Down the hall over there to the left!" There were still quite a few guys playing pool and sitting around at tables talking when I headed down the hall, my baggies tenting from my piss-hard-on! I had held the beers too long already. As I stood at the long metal trough trying to get the pee to start flowing, a biker guy stepped up beside me, fished out his dick, stroked it a couple of times before he started to piss. He was watching me standing, trying to get my hard-on down far enough to piss.

He said, "Got a little problem son - too hard to piss huh? Listen to my piss hit the metal and it may help!" Sure enough, as I listened to him take a long slow piss, I was able to get mine flowing. I let out a sigh of relief as my stream splashed into the trough and mixed with his. When his piss stopped and he milked it, I was looking right down at his dick. He just stood there stroking his dick watching me. When I gave my last final sprays and milked the last drops off the foreskin, he was still standing there slowly stroking his cock watching me. His dick was now hard, at least 8 inches of prime circumcised beef displayed to me. He turned facing me and said. "Touch it boy, you know you want to!" I did more than that! I was on my knees sucking on him in a quick flash. He blew in about ten good revolutions, depositing a hot load of jizz into my mouth. He shoved his dick back into his britches, zipped up and was gone that quick. I was left kneeling, licking my chops wanting more, lots more. I put mine away, zipped up, wash my face and hands with cold water thinking it would calm my nerves, possibly get the need to be screwed to calm down inside my ass. I made my way back, stopped and watched the guys playing pool for awhile, then returned to my stool. Dick was now behind the bar tending to customers and Mike was starting to clean up the bar!

Dick came over, stood behind the bar where I was sitting when he finished serving a couple of guys just as Duke plopped in the stool next to me. Dick pored a straight shot, downed it. He filled two more shot glasses. He dropped one each into two fresh drafts he had sitting on the bar and pushed them before Duke and me. Duke looked to be as horny as I was, pants bulging with manly desires. Duke said, "Maybe you two should have waited awhile before you took those Ecstasy pills boys. This may help you two male whores keep your cool for another hour or so. I put my hand on Dukes dick, gave the ten inches a squeeze, smiled at him and said, "Hello Big Guy - Is that a pistol in your pocket or are you just glad to see me?" He smiled, moaned and put his head on my shoulder, as I continued to play with his dick through the denim material of his tight pants, the wet spot grew where the head lay on his left thigh. He was excited and I knew I wanted him. I whispered in his ear, "Meet me in the back storeroom Duke and I can give you a quickie!" He would have followed me through the gates of hell by then he was so in need. Sure enough, there was a large storeroom in the back. A minute later he came in walking stiff legged. He wasted but two seconds, pulling his dick out and feeding it between my puckered lips. It was not big around, so it slipped right down my throat without a hitch. He humped my face for less than ten long strokes and dumped a load into me. He staggered back, still erect and said, "Do it again Joey!" I did! He blew again in record time and we straightened up and returned to our barstools. I noticed he was still semi-erect and oozing cum like crazy. His crotch was a dark shade of blue where his dick head continued to ooze.

That straight shot in my draft definitely calmed me a little, but my ass was still throbbing, just not as persistent as before. I put my nose to Duke and inhaled his scent, straightened up and said, "Duke, you smell good - nice and masculine! Give me some sugar handsome! "He pushed me away and said, "I don't kiss bitch - only pussy boys kiss each other! Don't try that again or I'll mess up that pretty face of yours! Now straighten up!" I looked at my watch and it was only 12:45am, thinking, "What in the hell are we going to do until 2:00am." Mike sat in a stool next to Duke and they talked as Duke fondled and massaged Mike's thighs and back. I found this quite boring to watch, actually more frustrating than boring, wishing it were I.

I hopped down off the barstool, went back and stood near the guys playing pool. Every once and awhile I felt a hand graze my ass. When I would look around at the guy, he would smile and pucker his lips at me, then go on playing pool. The guy I had blown in the bathroom returned from the bar with a draft and handed it to me, smiled and whispered. "Go in the bathroom if you want to suck some more dick boy." I looked at him, smiled and thanked him for the beer. When I finished that draft, I took the mug back to the bar then headed for the bathroom thinking how sweet it is to be so popular and surrounded by all these macho men. I was standing at the sink watching the door in the mirror when the big hunk that had been patting my ass at the pool table walked in. He wasted not a second as he ushered me into the furthest cubicle and sat me on the toilet. The doors on all three cubicles had been removed leaving us wide open for possible interruption. He stood over me, crotch at my eye level, opened his leathers, pulled his cock and balls out and ordered, "Suck it boy!" He never said another word all the time I was sucking him off, but he did moan and groan as he held my head firmly between his two hands and forcefully worked his dick where ever he wanted, mostly buried down my throat. He was hot and I brought him to a climax quickly, getting but a small taste of his massive juicer as it shot directly down into my stomach. He backed away, and another guy took his place immediately, cock already out and ready to go.

I serviced the two before I saw Duke standing at the entrance to the cubicle. He pulled me to my feet, glared at me and punched me hard in the stomach. I folded and dropped to my knees. He lifted me back up on my feet and back handed me across the face a couple of times and yelled, "What the fuck you doing in here, giving away our services boy! A quickie blowjob is $20. If they want you to suck on their balls, it is $30. Rim jobs are $50. Don't ever let me catch you giving anything we sell away again, and always get the money up front." He pushed my ass back down on the toilet lid. "You understand?" I answered, "Yes Duke! Sorry!" He continued, "Now clean up your face and get your ass back to the bar. If any of those dudes want services, bring them over to me before you do anything. I'll do the negotiating and make sure they only get what they pay for too."

I returned to the table where the first guy I blew, the one that bought me the beer was sitting. I looked right in his eyes and said softly. "Any more of your buddies want a blowjob it will cost them $20 up front. They will need to pay up front to my boss Duke, the guy sitting at the bar talking with Mike. You guys got my ass in trouble and I will pay for my mistake later! Tell them not to pay Duke so

Mike or Dick can see what is going on or they might kick us out of here since they already paid Duke for the two of us to spend the entire night with them."

He smiled up at me and said, "Oh, I see! Yea, they could get pissed off big time alright if they knew you were working the guys seeing as you are already in a business deal with them. I'll see if I can get you some more business discreetly boy. Want another beer kid?" I answered, "Sure, why not!" He rose to his feet, brought me another draft, turned and made the rounds talking to all the guys. It was not long and they were stepping up to Duke discreetly forking out their $20 when both Mike and Dick were busy taking care of business. Duke would motion me to go to the bathroom. I serviced another 6 guys and earned us another $120 before 2:00am. Duke handed me $60, 50% of my earnings. I smiled and said, "Thanks Duke!" He said, "You did well boy, you earned it!

From now on, you will be on a 50/50 basis. You are a real earner Joey!"

At 2:00am the place cleared of customers. Mike and Dick closed the place down, emptied the garbage, pulled the tape on the register, counted the cash and put it all in the office safe. We were ushered upstairs to their apartment. It was a large loft, with half walls dividing off a modern stainless steel kitchen, bathroom, bedroom and playroom. The guys lived well! The place was tastefully decorated in mostly leather and chrome furniture, a few very large natural wood cabinets housing TV, stereo, surround sound equipment, video and DVD, all with carved doors so they could be closed to hide the equipment. Dick led us right to the playroom. We were all told to take off all our clothing. When he was nude, he amazed me. He was covered with hair, a real Bear - even his back flowed with long black hair. There were tattoos all over him, even his thighs and calves, some big, others small. His appearance really turned me on – firm tight belly, abs to die for, all mounted on a big Bear frame. This guy exercised! The room was full of mostly exercise equipment, but had a huge king size bed in one corner with a black leather cover over it and cuff restraints with chains mounted on each of the four corners. Dick wasted no time in pushing me on to the bed and pouncing on me, playfully rutting me playfully. He was all over me, rubbing his nude body over my torso and limbs. His huge salami was oozing pre-cum and his hairy body was spreading his strong scent all over me. He obviously was not into bathing when I found a pit. That pit was too much, until I got a good taste. Then I went wild slurping. His full beard was like a big paintbrush spreading goodwill all over my inner thighs as his tongue and lips went right to work chewing and suck on my rosebud. Like Ludwig, he was a master ass eater. His tongue was a delight as it took total control of my lusting sphincter muscle. I just closed my eyes and enjoyed the attention to my bottom as I savored the smell and taste that lingered on my lips and face from his pit juices.

When I opened my eyes, Duke had Mike on the bed next to us and was feeding his dick into him doggy- style. I handed Dick the KY and huge rubber I had pulled from my baggies when I undressed and said, "Please grease me, put on the rubber and fuck me. Use the rubber Dick - safe sex please!" He hesitated, took them from me, greased his middle finger and put it into me right up to the palm. He worked over my prostrate gland for awhile, greased up two fingers and did it again. After he had three fingers working comfortably in me, he pulled a large can from under the bed, dipped his hand into it and spread the contents over his entire hand, wrist and up his arm to the elbow. He worked his entire hand almost into me, spinning it and spreading his fingers to loosen me. He had me moaning and begging him to fuck me by then, as his fingertips were poking my hard walnut. He did this for a long time as I loosened more, little by little. Finally, he gave a push and his entire hand popped into my ass. My sphincter clamped around his wrist and he worked it around and around. The fire shot through me, but the pleasure it gave far exceed the fireworks on my rosebud. He settled down behind me and slowly worked his hand in further and further, just a little at a time until I felt his elbow pressure against my buns. He then started slowly working his entire arm in and out, his hand working back and forth over my hard walnut. I oozed pre-cum each time his hand ran over that sensitive button. I was so full; I just succumbed to his pleasure and let him own my insides.

I opened my eyes and looked to the side. Duke and Mike were still playing doggie baby! Duke was intent on making Mike a bitch with litter, obviously dropping load after load of spunk into his bitch now that he had her in heat. Mike was rutting his ass back trying to get more and more of what he wanted to consume. Duke was sweating profusely. His now familiar scent filled my nostrils as it dripped over Mike's back. Dick was still pleasuring himself working his arm and hand inside me. He whispered to me, "You like this baby?" I answered, "Oh fuck yes, it is wonderful, but there is nothing like a big salami pounding my ass! Just fuck me silly Dick and put your sweaty scent all over my body. Damn, how I love a big dick like yours inside me, going ballistic, exploding, balls slapping against my ass. Please get your hand out of me and give me some of that big salami. Please dick me Dick!" He slowly pulled from me, cleaned his arm and hands with a towel. He crawled back up on the bed and looked down at me.

"You must give me head first Joey. I like to have the torpedo armed before I put him in the tube and fire him off." He crawled up, straddled me and said, "Open wide! Down the hatch girl! It's time to taste and swallow the big salami." He was not kind with that monster either. He forced it down my throat quickly. It spread my mouth open to the maximum before it curved and slid down my throat. This was not an enjoyable experience for me, though I was high as a kite on that Ecstasy pill, drunk and lusting for him. He reached for a shelf above the headboard and took the lid off a bottle. The familiar smell of amyl nitrate filled my lungs when he let me gasp for air. After a hit of that stuff, I didn't care what he did to my throat with his big salami. He worked it in and out, balls bouncing off my chin, giving us both hit after hit of amyl. He would reach over and give Mike and

Duke hits too. Finally he pulled from me, scooted down and lifted my legs up on his shoulders. He slipped the rubber on and guided the armed torpedo right down until the two big tail fins slapped against my ass. His hangers were like two big slabs of beef liver covering his extra large eggs as they slapped my ass. It was heavenly as the warmth of them paddled my ass cheeks. More amyl put me into a steady rhythm and I undulated and cooed for him. I tried to meet each thrust, but Dick was soon pounding away at such a wild, furious pace, it made it impossible. It was all I could do just to hold my hands against the headwall to keep my head from banging as he thrust. My mind was reeling at the wonderful sensations that rushed through my body. I had my own cock in a stranglehold trying to keep from ejaculating until he exploded. Dick continued this monumental assault on my asshole.

It seemed an eternity passed with Dick continuing to plow my ass with his massive torpedo. He leaned back on his knees, pulling my ass back with him. Then, amazingly, he grabbed onto my thighs and pulled me back even further against his hot, heaving body. Lifted off the bed, my legs slipped from his shoulders and were caught in the recesses of his arms. He held me tightly to his chest, his huge torpedo fully impaling my chute. I leaned forward against him, reached my arms up and grabbed the back of his neck. My head nestled against his neck sniffing his aroma. I felt his sweat dripping from his body running down between our bodies. With several loud grunts, I felt that familiar twitching and jerking feelings associated with a climax. Dick fired his torpedo and I felt the warmth gather within me, the wonderful jerking of him as his weapon took flight. I let my own fountain cover our stomachs with warm jizz. With the final spasm of his massive cock, Dick released his hold on my thighs and we both collapsed in a heap onto the bed. When his breathing returned to a more normal pace Dick sighed, "Joey Boy, you are one fantastic fuck boy!"

I looked to the side and Duke was still plowing Mike's ass, very close to another massive eruption. I looked at my watch and realized we best get going very soon if I was to be home by 5:00am. Just about then, Duke exploded into Mike again and rolled over on his side exhausted, dripping with sweat. I just put my nose to him and inhaled, licking him gently on the neck as both Duke and Mike got to their feet, kissed and left the room together. Duke rolled over on his back and let me lick and suck on him; he even raised his arms giving me access to his delicious pits. He was such a beautiful young man, I just cuddled up next to him until he said, "Let's get our shit together and get out of here. I'll have Mike call us a taxi, you get our cloths."

While we were riding back to Polk Street to let him off before it took me on home, he leaned over and gave me a peck on the cheek, handed me a business card. I looked at it. All it had on the cars was 'Duke's Stud Service and a telephone number.' He took it from me, turned it over, scribbled a Polk Street address on the back and handed it back to me. He looked at me and said, "Call or come by anytime Joey, I'll teach you the ropes and screw your hot ass too for free! We could make some big bucks together." He jumped out and the taxi took me home. I walked through the door at 5:40am, about 20minutes before grandma usually rises. I was tired and just wanted to crawl into bed and sleep, but knew I had to do breakfast or she would know something was wrong. I did turn on the computer and leave a message for Master Jake that I was sick and would not be able to come by for training today. I called his number and left the same message on his machine. I took breakfast with grandma, told her I would not be having lunch at home, cleaned up the dishes and kitchen, went up and cleaned out and soaked in the bathtub until the water turned cold. I crawled into bed, did not awaken until well after 3:00pm. I dressed, made a sandwich, did some laundry and waited for dinner at 5:00pm. As I was waiting, I did a lot of thinking about Duke and my escapades during the previous night. Damn he was hot. I guessed him to be about four years my senior, already very street wise. I knew I would be with him again soon!

CHAPTER 11

Having slept all morning and until 3:00pm Friday afternoon after lunch, after I had dinner with Grandma Schmidt and cleaned up the kitchen and dishes, I finally felt chipper again, full of piss and vinegar. Too much beer, the Ecstasy pill, and carousing all night had really drained me of all my energy. Sleeping all day and now with a stomach full of grandma's home made lasagna, I was hell bent on having some fun again as I did last night with Duke. Actually, what I really wanted was to be alone with Duke. I could not get him off my mind - such a sexy hunk and just a few years older than me. If I had to be a hustling whore for him to get him to molest me, be near me, want me around him, I guess that is what I would have to do - it was that simple in my mind! Sure, I had sucked him off twice in the back room of the bar, but what I really wanted was for him to make love to me, put his meat to me, immerse and flood me with his taste and scent. Like Trooper Jerry, I fell for him from the very first time I laid eyes on him. I had those feelings for him the minute I got a good look at him after he wrapped his arm around my waist at the corner of California and Polk last night.

A little after 7:00pm right after grandma went to bed, I telephoned the number on the card Duke had given me and his voice came on the line. "Duke's Stud Service, I'm not in right now, so leave your name and phone number and I'll get back to you A.S.A.P." It was a damn answering machine. I started talking, "This is Joey, wondered if you wanted some company tonight! You know what I want, or you should you handsome devil!" His deep masculine voice came on the line, "Well, what ever it is you want baby, you got it, but don't expect to get kissed darling!" He laughed and then continued. "Friday night Joey, busy night you know - the customers will be lined up looking for some big dicks and hot boy pussy. So, you want to make some more big bucks, right?" I answered, "Well, what I really want is your dick Duke, I thought maybe you and I could ..." He broke into my conversation, "Now look bitch, you want my dick you got to work for it. Get your hot ass over here pronto Joey boy! Don't give me a bunch of shit about all that mushy stuff you pussy boys want from me. You make us some money tonight and I'll give you plenty of meat, OK! Just spare me the sweet honey shit! I was just heading out the door when you called! Are you with me or not?" His dominant nature overwhelmed me. I responded, "Sure Duke, want me to meet you there or at the corner where I met you last night?" He said, "Come here first, put you in some sexy clothing, make you a real showpiece tonight for the Johns to drool over! Make it snappy - take a taxi - you got the address, right?" I answered, "Yes! See you in a jiffy dick head!" He said, "That's the spirit cunt boy!"

Thank goodness I had cleaned and bathed about 4:00pm. All I had to do was call a taxi and be on my way. When the taxi pulled up in front of the Poke Street address, I was looking at the mailboxes wondering what apartment he lived in, when suddenly he appeared on the front door landing and greeted me. "Joey, come in babe!" He put his arm around my waist, squeezed my ass and ushered me into the foyer, up the two flights of stairs and into his apartment on the third floor. Two young guys were sitting at a table eating fast food - another one was in the kitchen area. I recognized all from the street corner the night before. He said. "Joey, meet Jack, Paul and

Shawn." He pointed to each as he called their names. Another guy came walking down the hall toward us. He continued, "And this is Troy. Jack and Paul top only. Shawn and Troy bottom like you girl, great in bed too! They all work for Duke's Companion Services, just like you will be too real soon Joey!" He said, "Shawn, Troy, take Joey in the bedroom, dress him in something real sexy, but leave boxers and baggies on him. He looks hot in them pulled down low!" He motioned for both Shawn and Troy to me. Both were about my size. Shawn was a knock dead black haired beauty, Troy a very fair complexioned, pretty redhead. As for Jack and Paul, they were nice looking hunks, sporting huge baskets, the important commodity in any rich gay community of guys that liked them big, macho and rough looking. Each stood six-foot or better with hot bodies all dressed in worn denim and leather.

When Shawn and Troy finished with my makeover, they had me dressed in a skintight, solid light green, very short tank top. It only came down midway between my nipples and navel. They had me in a bright green pair of boxers. My light beige baggies hung off my hips a good two inches below the boxers. They had green and white runner shoes on me. To top it off, they put a short very tight, WWII light brown tailored leather pilot's flight jacket on me that they said should not be buttoned, just left draped open. They transferred all my little tubes of KY and rubbers from my jacket. Then they went to work on my face - a touch of blue eye shadow and just a dab of pink rouge on each cheek, and shinny, clear lip-gloss. They paraded me back to Duke and his eyes lit up. "Wow! That should turn their eyes! What a beauty, right guys?" Jack and Paul came over and ran their hands all over me. Jack even stepped up behind me, ran his hands up under my tank top, tweaked my nipples as he rutted me with his crotch, growled like a lion and said, "Fuck yes boss, he'll kill em dead!" Duke said, "OK boys, time to rumble, so take your pill and get to work and make some money tonight." He handed all four a little white pill. They went to the kitchen, washed it down with water and out the door they went.

Duke turned to me, led me to the kitchen, shoved a pill in my mouth and handed me a glass of water. "Down the hatch Joey, keep you from getting drunk and keep you awake for hours." After he got it down me I asked, "What was that pill Duke?" He answered, "Amphetamine, a Super Upper baby, keep you awake, feeling great, warm as toast in that skimpy outfit! We do not want you catching your death of cold do we! Come on, you will stick with me again tonight Joey!" When we reached the street, a taxi was waiting, and off we went. Along the route he talked, I listened. "Duke and Mike want us back at the bar tonight Joey. The guys have spread the word about you since last night. I hope they have a packed house - be like money in the bank. Sure beats working the streets or an 8 to 5! Might even be able to get Dick and Mike to spring for another fling too, especially with you dressed like this tonight! Oh La-La! You are one hot number! Wait until these guys feast their eyes on you Joey. I'll work the money and make sure they only get what they pay for! You just take your orders from me and get them off as quickly as possible! It's a numbers game. Understand! They get drunk and wild Joey, but most of them are nice guys, just looking for a good time with a pretty filly like you."

When we walked in the door Dick and Mike were both working behind the bar. The place was packed with bikers, leather dudes, longshoremen, and wharf and construction workers. Duke led me through the crowd right to the far end of the bar and took my coat off so everyone had a good view of me. The whistles and shouts said it all! Dick had already brought us a couple of beers with a shot-glass already sitting in the bottom of each draught mug. I turned to Duke and said, "There is no way I can service all these guys! Any way you can get in touch with Shawn or Troy, maybe both to get down here too?" He said, "Yea, I was thinking the same thing - the place is cooking alright." He pulled his cell telephone out of his coat pocket and immediately got through to Shawn. Troy was with a trick, but Shawn said he could be down in a few minutes. Dick said they had set up the back room with two mattresses, towels, lube and rubbers.

Duke said, "OK Joey, get out there and work the crowd. Let em get real friendly with you so they know what they are buying darling!" Dick held out his hand to me and said, "You better take this honey, you will need it!" He handed me an Ecstasy pill! I plopped it in my mouth, washed it down with the boilermaker and wrapped my arms around Duke, gave him a hug and said, "You know I'm doing this for you Duke, only because of you!" He answered, "I know baby - now go kill em boy and we will open for business in the back when Shawn arrives!" As I walked through the crowd of bears and macho muscle men, they had their hands all over me. Just about every guy in the place had his turn pulling my buns up against him, running his hands over my bare stomach and rutting my buns with his crotch. I finally had to protest, slap a few hands when my baggies and boxers were pulled down to my knees exposing everything to everyone. Before I could get my boxers and baggies pulled back up, guys massaged, pinched, even wet fingered my ass. These guys were wild animals. However, I was infatuated with the smell of these man beasts that surrounded me. I finally worked my way back to Duke and he kept them at bay, shaking his fists at them and shouting, "Back room 15 minutes guys - get your money out - prices are posted on the bulleting board!" Guys hovered around the sheet he had posted immediately checking service charges! The guys were getting restless shouting Joey, Joey, Joey, Joey; so Duke sent me back into the crowd again to be fondled, rubbed, goosed, and fingered. One big guy had me up on his shoulders carrying me around piggyback until others pulled me off him so they could play with of me too. I finally saw Shawn coming in the front door and making his way to the bar. I worked my way back to the bar again. Duke was setting up a payment cash box. Dick brought both Shawn and me another draft, handed an Ecstasy pill to Shawn and said, "The troops are getting restless, you two best get to the back and ready for a busy night." We looked at Duke awaiting his orders.

Duke finished with the cash box, turned to us and said, "Get up on the end of the bar here boys, strip for the guys, let them see what's for sale. Be sure and bend over so they see your pinkies, then hop down and go to the back room and I will follow to collect and tell you what

services to perform for each guy. We are officially open for business!"
I followed Shawn's lead as we hopped up and stripped, throwing our
few cloths to Dick behind the bar until we were completely nude. The
guys were howling, whistling and shouting. When we both bent over
in unison and spread our ass cheeks open for them to gander, the place
went silent for a moment. Then the stampede started as they came for
us. Duke stepped out and put his hands up, fists clutched. Dick quickly
jumped from behind the bar with a baseball bat in his hand tapping
it in one palm. The two of them escorted us to the back room where
Duke set the cash drawer on a small table and started sending them in
to Shawn and me two at a time giving us service instructions. Most
the guys had a pocket full of money having just had a payday, being
a Friday. They plugged out big bucks for our services. Duke charged
them all by the minute for anal sex. It kept the line moving faster. The
other services were set and displayed on the bulleting board. Some of
the guys came back three and four times before closing time. Most
of the guys wanted a blowjob; a few wanted their balls sucked too.
None paid the $50 for a rim job. However, we had 12 each that paid
for anal sex by the minute. The quick shooters were in and out in less
than three to five minutes, but we each had a few that worked us over
for over 20 minutes before they got their rocks off. Good thing Dick
brought more rubbers or we would have had a problem. Shawn and I
turned on with Ecstasy. That little pill made us into wantin' sluts. We
were having the time of our life sucking and fucking these animals,
our faces dripping with cum, our asses wantin' all we could get. That
magic pill really had us lusting for these guys, all sweaty, smelling
like masculine wild leather clad animals.

At 2:00am the bar closed, Duke counted the cash and kept half
and divided the other half between Shawn and me. The cash drawer
totaled $2,700. Duke gave Shawn and me both $675 each and kept
the other half, $1,350 for Duke's Companion Services. We called a
taxi and went back to the Polk Street apartment. Duke made me clean
out and shower before he would touch me. He said I smelled like a
cock slut until I showered. When he did usher me to bed, he gave
me everything I ever wanted from him. He fucked me steady from
2:30am until damn near 4:00am, before I fell asleep cuddled up with

his dick pressed against my buns. Thank god I had left that note for grandma in the kitchen telling her I had left early to catch the bus to the College for a Freshman Orientation that started very early! I was able to sleep all morning with Duke, in his bed, in his arms, getting his scent and body all over me. Like Trooper Jerry Gallagher, Duke liked it rough, and could fuck for hours. He did eventually peter out! We all had breakfast together about 10am. I followed him around like his puppy dog. He finally said something to Jack and Jack ushered me into his bedroom. The guy was hung very well and very wild in bed. He took to me and gave me exactly what I wanted. He wasn't Duke, but he knew how to make me scream with delight with his big fat dick. He rode me like a wild stallion, until my ass was tender and sore. I finally had to ask him to stop. I left for home about 1:30pm. Duke told me to be back tonight and we would kill em dead again! I told him, "I don't think so, not tonight Big Guy! He still would not let me kiss him on the lips before I left. I found that odd!

I made myself a BLT sandwich with a glass of milk and some potato salad before I went upstairs and checked for messages. I had one email from Master Jake. It was a get-well message and instructions to show up Monday morning at 10:00am to resume training with he and the Major. I used Big Red to clean out well and then soaked in a tube of hot soapy water for over an hour. I crawled under the covers and slept until 4:30pm. I had dinner with grandma at 5:00pm as usual, cleaned up the kitchen and I was back upstairs in my bedroom watching for lights across at Trooper Jerry's apartment as I searched the Internet. About 7:00pm the lights came on in his apartment and the magazine went up in his window. You know where I promptly headed after checking on Grandma!

He has learned how much I love to arrive when he is still in his uniform. Well he did not disappoint me this Saturday night. He must have seen me coming, as he even had on his helmet and the sexy mirror like sunglasses. I just stood in awe admiring him when he opened the apartment door. He stood there, legs spread wide, tapping his nightstick in his gloved hand and asked, "Where the fuck were you all night last night Joey? I saw you leaving in that taxi last night."

I lied and told him I went to a movie. I knew he didn't believe me, especially when I hesitated in coming up with a title for the movie, where it was playing. He said, "You were out whoring around you little tramp! Damn boy, what are you up to now, working the streets like a common hustler?" I answered, "No Sir! I met a new friend about my age and spent the night with him." As a police officer, he knew how to interrogate. When he got through asking me questions about my new friend, he knew I was not giving him the entire story. Why I gave him the Poke Street address is beyond me. It just came out along with the name Duke Brockman, the name I remembered on the mailbox from last night, in his questioning, He said, "I'll have him checked out. You best be telling me the truth Joey!" He pulled his cell telephone from his belt and called in the address and the name Duke Brockman requesting information. He listened intently as the answers came back. He disconnected from the terminal and replaced the telephone on his belt.

"Joey, Joey, Joey! This guy Duke has a long record of hustling and drug charges. He runs an outfit called Duke's Companion Services, constantly moving his operation around the city. He turns young runaways into male whores for him. They keep changing addresses in the Polk, Castro, and Mission Districts. Bad news Joey! Some friend you have found this time! Makes junkies out of his boys and gets them to whore for him. What am I going to do with you Joey?" I shrugged my shoulders and said, "Spank me, lecture me, and fuck me silly Sir?" He evidently did not like my smart-ass answer! He grabbed me by the shoulders and shook me until my teeth and bones rattled. He backed me against the wall and held me there with his nightstick to my chest as he backhanded me back and forth across the face with his other gloved hand. "Joey, what has gotten into you boy, have you lost your senses taking up with his kind! Imagine yourself picked up and hauled off in a paddy wagon some night found whoring for him. What do you think Grandma Schmidt, your dad and mom would think of you! Oh Joey, Joey, you are becoming a worry to me boy! I'm going to have to have a little talk with Grandma Schmidt or you parents if you don't get your shit together boy!" He kept poking me with that nightstick as he talked. I could not tell if he was more concerned about my safety than enraged that I was not exclusively his, but I knew better than make any more wisecracks.

He stepped up to me and put his entire weight against me. I was sandwiched between him and the hard wallboard. He kept banging me back against them with his body until he had the breath knocked out of me. I could not see his eyes through the mirroring sunglasses, just my own reflection. I knew what ever he was going to do with me it was going to be serious business. He worked my coat off and threw it on the floor, which was not like him. Everything in his abode normally had to be tidy, clean, dressed and covered. He was definitely out of character tonight. He grabbed my tee shirt at the collar with both hands, yanked it so hard it ripped from my neck. Two more hard yanks and it ripped from my body and lay on the floor. He didn't even bother to loosen the tie holding my baggies from slipping off me. His hands grabbed them on each side and he yanked them down in one aggressive move. The baggies and boxers lay at my ankles. He ordered, "Well kick them off boy, the runners too," leaving me in my white socks, nothing more. He put his boot toe on the end of my sock and held the cloth to the floor. "Pull your foot out boy! He did the same with the other sock" Now I was completely nude, held against the wallboard not knowing what to expect from him next.

"What you smirking at boy? You spout off that smart mouth of yours again and I'll wipe it off your face pronto! Nothing seems serious to you Joey. This whoring around has to stop!" I couldn't help myself. I snickered and grabbed for his basket and gave it a squeeze licking my lips. He had a huge hard-on; his pants were about to split open from pressure alone on the twill material. He jumped back, loosened his Sam Brown Equipment Belt, buckled it back together and hung it around my neck. It was loaded with equipment, heavy, bulky and pulled down on my neck. He loosened his regular uniform belt, opened his pants, the white boxers and lifted his genitalia completely free. His excited, hard dick flopped up against his stomach; balls hung as bulls' huge gonads from his crotch. He stood there stroking himself and said. "Look at this Joey. Isn't it enough to keep you happy baby?" I want you all to myself Joey! I do not want anyone else fucking with you - NOBODY JOEY! Now pick up this mess, come in the bedroom and finish undressing me properly. I purchased a few new toys today that should put a smile on your face since you like rough sex and kink so well." I hesitated, just mesmerized at this picture of masculine perfection before me. "I SAID, MARCH YOUNG MAN AND I'LL SHOW YOU I MEAN BUSINESS - MOLD YOU INTO MY LITTLE COCK SLUT! YOU ARE MINE JOEY - ALL MINE!"

As always, he had me undress him, hang his uniform, equipment and put his boots on the rack. Normally, he smelled manly, but clean always. Today he smelled raunchy once the clothing was off him. He had obviously not bathed for a couple of days. This was definitely not like him at all. He realized I noticed and commented, "Like my new aroma huh Joey! Well, I've been saving these smells just for you, knowing you like them so well. I have a very special treat for you too tonight." He walked up to me, shoved me down on to my knees, and pulled my face into his crotch. My head swam with the smell of animal, man beast and urine, a wonderful combination that I learned to like in the back room of the bar the last couple of nights. I just inhaled and rubbed my face in the intoxicating mixture. He could see my excitement. He placed his foot against my crotch and played with my rising rod getting me really turned on to him and said, "Pull the hood back now Joey for your surprise!" As my hand drew the long umbrella off the head, another familiar smell filled my head. The head covered with small white specks, the glands had a big ring of white smegma covering them. He must not have cleaned his dick for two or three days to have gathered this much headcheese under his foreskin. I just looked at it in disbelief, inhaling the raunchy smell. He whispered, "Joey, your dessert! Taste it - saved it all for you! Knowing you Joey, you will love it!" I gave him no indication I had done this before, but I put my tongue out and gathered just a few flecks and made him think it was my first taste. It tasted so good! I looked up into his eyes and said, "Mmmm Daddy - tastes like cheese – SO GOOD!" I immediately stuck my tongue in the big circle of white, rolled my tongue around his glands, coating my tongue with the substance. I held my tongue out, looked up at him and smiled, spread the white all over my lips and slowly licked it a little at a time into my mouth. The look on his face was one of complete wonderment. He responded, "What ever turns you on Joey - I'm here to make you happy baby! I had a feeling you would like it!" I was so busy savoring the smell and the flavor of him His eyes were ablaze with lust, white teeth gleaming down at me as he said, "Tell Daddy thank you for the dessert he saved for you."

"Thank you Daddy - tastes like the Limburger Cheese dad and I use to eat when I was younger. Dad and I loved it; mom thought it was horrible smelling, even worse tasting. She didn't want it in the house; so, dad and I would go on Saturdays to the cheese store, buy it, and eat it before we arrived home. She always knew though, because the smell kind of hangs around for awhile, gets on your breath and lingers for hours. This brings back wonderful memories of being with my dad. Yes, I love it Daddy - save me more!" I went back looking for more, anything I may have missed. I found quite a few more drops of white to consume. He just looked down, smiled and chuckled to himself and said, "My little Cock Slut - look at him go for the cheesy smegma. I was so caught up in eating his head cheese I dropped from my knees and sat with my legs out in front of me and scooted down under his ball sack and sucked on them. They hung off him like slabs of raw steak - exciting to touch, delicious to taste, smelling raunchy too. I spun around on my ass and licked up his perineum, that rough cord of skin that connects his two halves running between his balls and his ass hole. He spread his legs, lowered himself slightly and spread his ass cheeks as I slowly moved up between his ass cheeks. The moist hair, ass smells increased as my tongue floated back and forth over the rough tissue exciting my tongue and lips. He leaned forward so his hands could spread his buns, and his hairy trough opened up enough for me to continue licking and sucking right up to his pucker hole. Framed in a solid mass of moist ringlets of hair, it was breathtaking to my lustful eyes. The mixed scents of his man scent and anal juices filled my nostrils. My tongue followed my eyes right to the pucker and darted out for my first real taste. It tasted even better than the smell. I was captivated instantly and my lips sucked it in as my tongue darted, spooning the tasty delight.

"Oh yes Joey Baby! Eat daddy's ass! Lick and nibble on Daddy's butthole. Show him how much you love him baby! Now you are truly Daddy's little butt-licker too!" Suddenly, he let out a big fart that rattled my lips, not a real stinker, but definitely a noisemaker. Startled at first, then amazed at the feelings it put on my lips. I loved it as it rattled against my lips. I begged, "Oh, do it again Daddy - that was awesome!" I attached my lips to his anus and he let out another big one, rattling my lips even more. I just moaned as he let a few smaller ones. He commented, "You like that huh baby - ain't you something! Spin around here now and suck on daddy's big hard dick for awhile, see if we still can get it down that tight throat again."

He straightened back up; legs still spread, put his hands on the back of my head and guided his member into my mouth. Being as large as he was, naturally his dick was hard from my anal antics, but not rock hard. It took a lot of blood to keep something as big as his dick rock hard. It was still pliable, slipped over my tongue and down my throat without too much trouble, except for the girth of the monster. I had sucked enough big dicks at the bar the last two nights, I had no difficulty with his tonight. He whipped that big baby down my throat until his knees began to shake. I felt his spunk surging up his shaft just as he pulled back and it emptied over my tongue so I would get the full taste over my taste buds. It was delightful; his juices were always so runny and sweet tasting. As I looked up into his eyes, he smiled down at me, held my head in place and I soon had a warm stream of his bladder fluids filling my engorged mouth. I was very careful not to loose a single drop on his bedroom carpet. I even cleaned and sucked his hood dry and clean, knowing he would insist I do so before I released his manhood.

"OK Joey, you did well boy! To bed with you now, until I get my second wind." He crawled up next to me, put his hand over my body and told me to jack off into his hand. I wanted more, but at least he didn't make me try to go to sleep all horny. After I dropped my load into his hand, he put it to my mouth and said, "Clean it up Joey and I'll fuck you baby after awhile! Daddy won't deprive you of that reward for giving him such a terrific blow-job tonight baby!"

CHAPTER 12

Before I fell asleep, my ass pushed up against Trooper Jerry Gallagher, my mind started to work overtime thinking about what he had said to me about being his boy, only his boy. Was this what I wanted? No, it was what he wanted. I loved the big guy, but no more than I loved Master Jake and the Major, the Skinheads Blake and Ludwig, even Big Black Amos, or the hustlers Duke and Jack. I loved them all equally, well almost equally. Was he going to start getting possessive of me? Sure sounds like it! I milled this over in my mind for awhile and came to the conclusion I liked and wanted things to continue just as they were at present. I also realized that all my favorite guys had big dicks; so, I determined that was the common denominator attracting me to them. I had heard the term size queen, so I settled on the fact that that is what I must be too, a Size Queen. Hell, they could be handsome or ugly, smart or mentally challenged, or rich or poor, I did not care as long as they had a huge dick on them and they knew how to work it up my ass and make me feel so fucking good. Nothing else compared to how absolutely fantastic it made me feel, and here I was only 18 years old already well addicted to sucking cock and wild, rough anal sex. Of course, my sex partner had to be dominant, masculine and all man right to the core. What made me like sex with men at this early age I had pondered for weeks now? The answer finally came to me as clear as clear can be once Trooper Jerry began calling me Baby. I knew now why I liked having sex with men, especially those with a strong masculine smell and forceful aggressive nature in their lovemaking.

As a young boy taking a hot soapy bath with my dad, sitting up between his legs in the bathtub, his big long dick would always be up against me, against my back or resting in the crack of my ass. Many a time he would get hard, rub it against me, hold me to him tightly, kissing the top of my head, playing with my little nipples, softly calling me his Baby Boy, rubbing my thighs with warm soapy water with his big hands until he would start moaning softly in my ear. Eventually his whole body would stiffen, convulse and undulate against my body as he held me tightly against him and whispered words in my ear I had never heard before or understood. I could feel the warmth of his ejaculation as his juices covered my back and his hard dick pulsated up between the two halves of my little butt. Right from the beginning he would gather the warm nectar with his fingers and rub it over my lips until he had me licking and tasting his juices. Once he realized I liked his nectar he taught me to blow him in the tub or shower until mama caught me with his big cock in my mouth and him working a finger up my ass as he played with my little hard cocklet. I use to treasure those moments being close to my dad and smelling him before his scent was bathed away. His strong scents I still remember even though I was too young to realize it was something sexual. Those images of him still occupied my mind in detail after all these years. Have I really been attracted to big men, the strong masculine smell of them, and being touched, rubbed and used sexually by them because of my love for my dad and what he would do with me until that night when mama caught him playing sex games with me? Needless-to-say he never bathed me or let me see, play or taste his Yum-Yum toy again.

I awoke to the feel of Trooper Jerry slipping the meat to me. He was slobbering on my neck, slowly pushing into me. His cock snot was lubing me enough that he just slipped in paving the way to my hot spot. By now, he knew exactly where that baby nut lay within me. Once his dick head reached that spot I was instantly excited and began pumping back against him. He knew what I liked and he was giving it to me. He whispered, "Don't dare shoot and mess up the bed Baby! Squeeze it off if you have to, but do not dare make a mess in my bed. You are going to have to learn control or I will have to keep a rubber on you at night! I can't be changing bed sheets every time I fuck you during the night!" I said, "Brilliant idea Sir, hand me a rubber so I can shoot with you and really twitch my muscles when you explode!" He reached back, grabbed another rubber and said, "Here, let me do it!" He slipped it over my hard cock, gave it a couple of strokes and went right back to rutting me, and could he ever rut and hump my ass! His big fat dick really fit snuggly and knew exactly how to deliver unbridled pleasure along the walls of my love canal. He was a real dominant when it came to pleasuring himself with my body. He always bit, chewed, nipped and sucked, hands constantly traveling over me. I always ended up just thrusting, squeezing my ass to get more of his pleasures; as he loved to have me constantly in lust for him during intercourse. Tonight was no exception. I gave myself to him, became his submissive wild bitch, and rode him hard and long before he brought us both to a raging climax. I put a nice load in my rubber.

No sooner had we recovered from that rutting than he withdrew from me and said, "To the playroom Joey, I have some new toys I want to try on you. Leave the rubber on too full of your spunk. It becomes you dangling between your legs! We will see if we can fill it up tonight!" He led me into what I knew as his weight room, study. I stood in amazement how he had converted it into a weight room play room. He had removed the old carpeting, right down to the old hardwood floors. The ten-foot cove ceiling nearly touched a four-posted framework that supported a dungeon harness dangling from ropes attached to small, chrome, block an tackles attached to the structure. It was massive, well made with 4x6 and 4x8 lumber with carriage bolts holding it together. It was free standing and looked as though it might be used. He said, "Well, this should be fun for us! I purchased it for little or nothing from a friend that moved out of his apartment into a house! Now wait until you see what else I bought! He pointed to a big wooden Armoire. He led me over to the Armoire, opened the door and he had it full of S&M paraphernalia. Most looked used also; however, some was obviously new. I noticed he had an electric stimulating device in the cabinet, whips, cuffs, both leg and wrist restraints. He had damn near as many devices and items as Master Jake had in his full-fledged dungeon. There was a gruesome set of nipple clamps, ball gag, a leather hood, and a cock and ball spreader. Hanging off the inside of the left door was a Cat-of-nine-tails. A chill ran through me as I stared at it remembering my first taste of one of those in Master Jake's cold dungeon. I noticed he had two bottles of amyl nitrate on one of the shelves. I asked, "You into S&M too Sir? You have some pretty heavy duty stuff here!" He smiled! "You are soon to find out Joey!"

He put wrist and leg restraints on me, the ball gag and led me over to the harness apparatus. He had me lay back into it and hooked up the big D rings so that I was suspended off the floor, face up, legs and arms spread out wide. He pulled on a couple of ropes and readjusted me so my legs were pulled up toward my chest, leaving my ass open and attracting his eye about level with his groin. I seemed comfortable in this position, my weight evenly distributed in the harness. He put the huge nipple clamps on me. Their bite put tears in my eyes. To make it worse, he yanked on them a couple of times with the chain that connected them watching me squirm in pain. He took a long piece of what looked to be leather shoelace, found the center by holding the two ends together, tied that center on to the center of the nipple chain. He pulled the chain taunt with the two leather ends and tied them off in the D rings that held my wrists up over my head. He tested his masterpiece by swinging the harness gently. Each revolution pulled, sending more pain to each nipple. Even after he stopped swinging me, any movement of my wrists tweaked the nipples. First he stood back with a big feather and tickled me on the bottom of my feet. I am especially ticklish there and as I jolted it started me swinging from the tall framework. Each swing caused the nipples to pull away from my chest with considerable pain. The ball gag kept me from yelling or screaming four letter words at him. He just moved that feather all over me, smiling having a good time. The more I struggled, the greater the pain to my nipples. Secondly he lined himself up with my bottom, pushed Almighty into me and began to rut me gently. The rutting was feeling very good, but the action on my nipples was still very painful. As his excitement increased, so did both my excitement and pain. I started to hum and hum I did, hoping the pain on my nipples would stop. As my humming increased, so did his thrusting. Soon my nipples went from sore and painful to warm and pleasantly erogenous. He smiled at me and said, "Starting to feel real good huh baby," as he really put the meat to me. I was humming, eyes glazed over looking up into his beautiful face when he shouted, "Skeet for me baby, make those ass muscles pulsate!" I shot another load of Cub Boy Juice into the rubber and he exploded. He was dripping with sweat as he leaned over me letting the harness and apparatus support both our weight. My nose twitched as his aroma filled my head.

"You liked that baby! Really got you going!" He pulled from me, inserted a huge dildo into me and hooked it up to an electrical cord. When he switched it on, I just lay spread eagle enjoying the pleasure. He gave me a gentle push getting me swinging and my nipples warmed right back up. He walked away saying, "Have fun with it baby, I'll be back shortly!" I found that I was able to control my swing by either pushing with my ankles or pulling with my wrists. I could have swung forever with this warmth spreading through my entire body. I kept putting more cream in my rubber as I had one climax after the other. My entire body became an erogenous zone. I found myself swinging as hard as I could to bring myself to another climax. I have no idea how long he was gone, but it did not matter. I was in a little world of my own giving myself pleasures I had under my total control. When he did come back into the room, it wasn't until I felt him licking and biting on my inner thighs that I opened my eyes and came back to earth just enough to enjoy this new sensation. It made me tingle all over, the constant nipping, his hot tongue stroking and lathering my skin with his moist saliva. The swinging action had stopped, but I was still able to pull on my nipples with my wrists. This was paradise indeed! He could see my pleasure and was also having his own slurping on my smooth white thighs. He eventually sucked and licked on my balls, as he became more excited seeing me so excited and turned on.

Suddenly he stopped, stepped to the cabinet and returned with additional pleasure giving items. When he had it all hooked up he flipped the switch and electrical stimulation started on my nipples. He took the ball gag out of my mouth and I moaned and cooed for him, as the pleasure was unbelievably wonderful. He stood to the side so I could again swing myself. He stood and watched me with the electrical control in his hand increasing and trying the different settings to give me maximum pleasure. He pushed a couple of buttons and it began to send different random voltages to my nipples. When he was satisfied with his settings he sat it down, pulled the vibrating dildo from my rear and entered me again. He was very excited and became a rutting animal taking his pleasure with my hot pussy. When he came this time, he pulled his rubber off, put the open end to my lips and squeezed the contents into my mouth. Then he smiled down into my eyes and gave me his lips to nurse for a spell, darting his tongue in and out of my wantin mouth. I did not want this pleasure to end as he started to disengage all the paraphernalia and lower me back on to my feet. He told me to clean up the mess and put the toys back in the cabinet and meet him in the bathroom when I was done. He had a hot bath running for me as I joined him and told me to soak well or I would be sore later. That Saturday night was a memorable one as I fell asleep in his fold until early morning Sunday, only to return home alone and already lonely for my Trooper Jerry Gallagher's affection, lust and aroma.

I had promised grandma last week I would go to church with her Sunday morning. We went to the early 7:00am Mass service. She stayed with her friends and I returned and went immediately to see if Trooper Jerry was home. I had forgotten to ask him if he had this weekend off. There was no answer to my eight rings to his apartment buzzer. It was a beautiful sunny day. I went home up to my room and changed into casual clothing and decided to walk down to the Marina and watch the wind surfers that were always there on warm Sundays. At 8:45am, I hit the sidewalk walking toward the Marina, when an old Lincoln Sedan pulled up and both Duke and Jack jumped out and pushed me into the back seat. Duke jumped in next to me, Jack behind the wheel and sped off. Duke had a power lock on my wrist so I could not jump out until Jake hit the power locks. I used my other arm to reach for the door lock, but it would not disengage. Jack had evidently also set the child safety lock so only the driver could unlock the rear doors. It was not until then that Duke released his grip. He turned toward me and shouted, "Bitch, where were you last night? You realize how much business you cost me!" He backhanded me across the face until tears ran from my eyes. I almost felt my face swelling from the force of the blows. "I thought I made it quite clear to you that we were to be back at the bar last night. Thank god, both Shawn and Troy were available when you didn't show. You have to learn that business comes before pleasure. When I get through with you today, you will know the meaning of business, serious business." I did not know how to react, other than reminding him that I had told him I would not be back Saturday night before I left his place. That is not what he wanted to hear! He backhanded me a couple more times and said. "You fuckin' little bitch; leaving us out on a limb like that last night! What's wrong - wasn't a 50/50 split, $675 enough for your one night? Jack, go back to the apartment. You are far too valuable to me to think you can give me the slip that easily. When I get through with you today you will know that I am the boss and in total control of you Bitch!"

When they finally got me up into the apartment, kicking and fighting them all the way, I was held down by Jack as Duke tightened a rubber hose around my arm and put a needle to me. I almost immediately relaxed and my head began to swim. Hell, what ever was in that syringe was powerful stuff. I just lay there drooling, hardly able to speak. Duke said, "That should hold her for awhile! You first Jack, show him what we do with pussy boys that try to slip from my control." They had me rolled and disrobed in seconds. Jack pulled the butt plug from me, shoved his dick in me and fucked me relentlessly

as I slipped in and out of reality, almost comatose at times. Duke
kept asking me to repeat these words, "I'm your fucking bitch Duke,"
as Jack fucked me. Every time I would slip away into space I was
jarred awake and Duke would ask, "Who are you bitch. If I failed to
answer him with, "I'm your fucking bitch Duke," he lifted my head
up and shouted the question to me again until I answered. This went
on for what seemed like forever. The pleasures that Jack was giving
my bottom became so intense I was lusting with his every thrust.
When I would not answer Duke's question, Jack would pull from me,
leaving me with a void within that I really craved. He would not put
his dick back in me until I responded properly to Duke. I eventually
kept repeating, "I'm your fucking bitch Duke," to keep Jack rutting
me. Over and over, time after time, I responded just to keep that big
dick pleasing my need. When Jack was sweating, dripping wet from
the exercise, he rolled off and Duke took over. Hours later, I was
still muttering "I'm your fucking bitch Duke!" They finally tied me
and left me on the bed, begging for more dick, screaming, "I'm your
fucking bitch Duke, please fuck me! Please fuck me!" I finally fell
asleep! When I awoke, still tied, but now gagged also, I noticed a
digital clock on Duke's nightstand. It read 12:35pm, so I knew I had
been here for well over 3 hours already. I tried to get my bindings
undone but was unsuccessful. I did manage to roll off the bed on to
the floor making a loud thud.

Duke came storming into the room, both Jack and Paul on his
heals. Duke said, "Well how's my little cock slut feeling - all chipper
wanting another shot and some more fun with the boys by the look of
you?" He turned to Jack and Paul and said, "Get him back up on the
bed and hold him still!" He pulled the syringe out again as Jack held
me down, Paul tightened the rubber tubing around my arm, and Duke
gave me another shot. As before, I floated into a state of helplessness,
almost comatose, but this time aware of what was going on around
me. They untied and took the gag off me as Duke gave them orders.
"Paul you take a snort dude and fuck our little buddy here for awhile."
He handed Paul a straw and held the glass panel as Paul snorted a line
of white powder. He let out a roar like a lion and was nude in a flash.
Duke continued, "Roll him over and put this plastic under him or he

will be messing my bed up with cock-snot this time around with snow on his prostrate. OK, that should do it boys! Now dampen your dick head Paul and dip it into the Coke and we will make a real cock slut out of our new addition to the business! This should get him shooting cock-snot like the pretty little whore he is for sure!"

Jack spat in his hand and spread it over his huge dick and dipped the entire dick into the bowl of Coke until it was covered with the white powder. He crawled up and shoved it up my canal and rubbed it back and forth over my prostrate, buried it in me and went right to work fucking me like a wild man. He was even bigger than Jack or Duke. Again Duke started asking me, "Who am I?" I knew the response he wanted and whispered him correctly. "I'm your fucking bitch Duke!" He whispered back, "I can't hear you darling! Who am I boy cunt?" I spoke up, "I'm your fucking bitch Duke, you fuckin asshole!" He lifted my head, looked down into my eyes and said, "Yea bitch, asshole maybe, but you're still my bitch, now say it again correctly!" He backhanded me across the face again and waited for my amended response. Out it came, "I'm your fucking bitch Duke!"

It was not long and my ass was aflame with wonderful new feelings I have never experienced before. Not just my slut button, but my entire pussy was on fire with a need only a man cock can deliver. I would have screamed anything they wanted to hear to keep that dick plunging inside me. I was oozing, and then started cumin streams, having multiple climaxes - convulsing and rutting my ass back over Paul's huge dick. Duke lifted my head and looked down into my eyes and said, "Baby, enjoy the great perks that come with your new profession darling. This shit will keep you coming back for more and more darling - Duke's pretty little cock slut in action taking care of us guys and making money for Daddy Duke! You will soon learn your position well baby and make me proud to have you on my team!" He leaned over and licked my face leaving a trail of his spit to dry up one side and down the other. He spread my lips with his thumb and forefinger, stuck his fuck finger in my mouth, dampened it and returned it covered with the magic white powder to my mouth and let me suck it for awhile. Paul's sweating body dripping with his wonderful scent continued rutting, as he were a well tuned machine. Duke dipped his wet finger in the white powder twice more, poking it up into each of my nostrils. My head went wild and my body convulsed in sheer ecstasy. He looked into my eyes again, smiled and said, "Look at this handsome face darling, and tell me who you are again Baby Doll!" I could hardly speak until he slapped me again! "I'm your," and I went blank for a moment. He repeated, "YOU'RE WHAT BITCH?" Another slap and I said, "I'm your fuckin bitch Dukie!" He smiled, "That's right Bitch - Dukie's little Bitch you are indeed!" He dropped my head back down on the sheet and addressed Paul and Jack. "Don't give him any more Coke for now boys. That should keep him real happy for awhile. Just keep giving him pleasure and having him tell you who he is over and over. When Paul peters out, Jack you start on him again and keep him awake." Duke climbed off the edge of the bed and left the room.

While Duke was out of the room, Jack snorted two lines of Coke, coated his dick with Coke as Jack had done, pushed Jack off me and mounted me. He went ballistic humping me and the coke spread inside me again drawing warmth and pleasure as before. I just floated in paradise dropping load after load of my spunk between my belly and the plastic, creating a cum-slick that was spread all over my groin causing even more pleasure for me. Eventually I ran out of spunk, but I continued to have one dry organism after the other as he dumped loads of his warmth into me. They kept me awake, repeating who I was until I just chanted those five words, "I'm your fuckin bitch Duke!" My head filled with that beautiful sentence by the time Duke reappeared holding my head in his hands prying my eyes open with his fingers. "You in there baby - talk to me Joey Baby - tell me who you are? I came out of my fantasyland slowly. Another slap across the face brought me back more quickly. I said, "What??? Oh yes, who am I Duke! No Duke, I mean, I'm your fuckin bitch Duke! Yea, that's what I want to be. I'm your fuckin bitch Duke and love taking care of your boys for you." He smiled at me again, kissed me on the forehead and said, "Yes, you're mine now Joey, Dukes new little druggie cock slut and money maker!" He kissed me again on the forehead and ordered the guys to take a break and grab something to eat in the other room."

He put one knee on the bed and rolled me over on my back where I could watch him. He helped me to sit on the side of the bed and wiped his fingers into my spunk-covered belly with his fingers. He put his fingers to me lips and told me to lick them clean. He sat down next to me, removed his shirt and smiled at me. He put his fingers back in my spunk and brought them back and rubbed then back and forth across my lips and said, "You love me now Joey, smell me, put your nose on me and smell me baby. It's a smell you will always crave, just inhale deeply and taste of me too! Go ahead baby, lick and taste. You will crave my smell and taste from this day forward baby!" I put my nose to his shoulder inhaled and licked. His salty taste covered my tongue. He lifted his arm and said, "Get a good smell and taste of me baby in my hairy armpit! Lick it nice and dry Joey; remember the smell and taste. It is going to be what you live for from now on Joey; I will take care of you and keep you happy forever and you will do what ever I ask of you from now on!" He rose and lifted me, put his arm around my waist and led me slowly out of the bedroom into the kitchen and fed me slices of finger food with his fingers until I turned my head away. He led me to the refrigerator, still holding my wobbly body, pulled out a cold beer, popped the lid and took a couple of swallows, then put it to my lips and held it while I drank. He kept looking into my eyes and smiling, rubbing my back and ass cheeks as I finished off the beer. I didn't realize just how thirsty I was until I started to drink. He somehow knew I was dehydrated from the session, as he pulled another beer out and put it to my lips. I gulped it down almost empty before I pushed it away. He finished it off then led me down the hallway to his bathroom, drew a hot bath and helped me in. He said, "There are boxes of Fleet Enema in the cabinet Joey, so clean your ass well so Duke can eat some pussy! Soak Joey, bathe and come back in the living room so I can take you to the bedroom, let you undress me and I will make love to my new beauty! Don't be too long, Duke is hungry for that beautiful body of yours' darling!" I looked at the clock and it read 3:14pm. I said, "I have to be home for dinner at 5:00 sharp Duke or we are all fucked!" He looked at his watch and said, "No problem baby, if you hurry in the bathroom - give us a good hour to make love and fuck around!"

I cleaned out well, jumped in the tub, took a nice hot bath and felt much better about my position in his eyes. I obviously had not considered what he was doing to me as I rushed back into his arms was led to his bedroom. He snorted two lines of Coke and rutted at me before he handed the straw to me and told me to snort a line. I coughed and almost choked, but I did it! This shit was powerful and all my defenses tumbled down again as I almost ripped his clothing off to get to his body. He smiled and laughed at my reaction to the drug. "He whispered, "You sure are a hot little bitch Joey - just looking at you turns me on! Start with the armpits, then work over the nipples!" I inhaled his pit, licked the hairy cavity, then the other. I was intoxicated sniffing, licking and enjoying his beauty. By the time I got to his nipples, I was lusting for him. He moaned, "Harder baby, I like my nipples nipped and tugged on baby boy! OH YEA - YOU GOT IT NOW BABY!" His cock sprung to attention and cock-snot dripped from the end of his umbrella. He had one of those cocks that the hood needed pulled back manually even when it was hard. I loved the look of it all hard and tented. I watched it grow and expand as I licked and nibbled my way right down to the beautiful hooded monster. I sucked the juice from beneath the hood, rolling my tongue around tasting his Smegma buildup. I muttered, "Oh good, head cheese," and buried my tongue back in and rolled it around and around again. I looked up with my eyes and he was smiling down at me, hands on his hips enjoying my enthusiasm. While my tongue was still inside his sheath, I gently pulled it back and the delicious smell of Limburger filled my nostrils. I lapped up the white specks and rolled them in my mouth against the roof of my mouth to get the full flavor. I sucked the head into me mouth and worked it back against my larynx then swallowed and inhaled the entire shaft down my throat. He began the motions as my throat muscles pulsated with anticipation. He let out a big moan and started pumping my throat and quickly dropped his load right down into my esophagus on its' journey to my stomach. He pulled from me and I licked his head skirt clean and dry with my lips.

I had prepared myself in the bathroom with a tube of KY I found in a drawer. He dipped his cock-head into the bowl of Coke, eased me back onto the bed, lifted my legs up on his shoulders and slipped right into me and began the ritual. The Coke took a few minutes to penetrate my anal membranes, but when it did, I went wild. He plowed, spaded and harrowed, preparing me for his seed. His hands grabbed and lifted my ass cheeks right up over him when he eventually spread his seed. He wanted me to stay for another plunge, but I looked over at the clock and it was going on to 4:20pm. I pointed to the clock and said, "I have to be home by 5:00pm sharp Duke and I have an appointment at 10:00am in the morning. Can someone drive me home?" He answered, "Sure Joey, but let me give you something to help you sleep tonight or you will be pacing the floor all night baby!" He pulled a big leather box out from under his bed and landed me four pills. He said, "Take one of the white ones tonight to sleep and if you feel like shit in the morning take the white ones with the cross on them and you should be OK. If not give me a call at this cell telephone number and I'll pick you up and fix you up with another shot! He handed me the card with both his cell and regular number on it. Just remember, you are going to be very nervous for a few days until your system adapts to the new drug in your system! Come to me when you cannot cope! You be back here tomorrow after your appointment. If not I'll just have to come and get you again. Understood Joey Boy?" I answered, "Yes Duke!" He said, "Now tell me who you are again Joey!" I looked into his beautiful eyes and said, "I'm your fucking bitch Duke!" He kissed me on the forehead and had Jack drive me home. I talked with Jack as we drove along. He welcomed me aboard, told me I was one hot pussy boy and I could be his anytime if Duke didn't want me as his bed partner. It made me feel special too as he pulled me up close to him and put my hand over his crotch and play with his manhood as he drove along slowly. I had him stop and let me out at the end of the block just in case Trooper Jerry was home and watching for me out his window.

I ate like a kid with two hollow legs at dinner that night, putting away the food. I made a real pig out of myself shoveling down grandma's beef stroganoff. I also drank a full quart of milk plus two pieces of apple pie. I was stuffed, but felt great until about 9:30pm. I came down quickly, cramps, headache, nausea and the sweats. What was happening to me? I heaved up my dinner and paced the floor for awhile before I took the pill Duke told me to take so I could sleep. That pill finally calmed me down and I fell asleep and slept right through until after 7:00am, only awaking then because grandma was banging on my bedroom door hollering, "Joey, you OK in there baby, breakfast is nearly ready?" I answered, "Be right down grandma!" I felt like hell again, half-asleep, half-awake with a pounding headache and a very sore bunghole. I was not feeling too well until after I put some food back in my stomach. I was careful not to overeat; thinking that must be what made me loose my dinner last night. After breakfast, I still did not feel much better. I did as Duke told me and took the two white pills with the cross on them. Before long, I was feeling great again.

The guy certainly knew his medicines. I thought, maybe he should become a pharmacist assistant. I warmed right up feeling very good. About quarter to 10:00am I made my way to Master Jake's house. A note was hanging on the front door indicating he had to rush to a family crisis and would not be back from Denver until Thursday or Friday afternoon. He would send me an email when he was back. I went back home feeling great until about lunchtime, then the cold sweats and the cramps began to start again. After lunch I gave Duke a call and told him everything that happened to me, including loosing my dinner, the cramps, the cold sweats and the nervousness and the raging headache. He said he would send Jack over to pick me up, as he had the magic potion that would make me feel well again almost instantly. By the time Jack picked me up the cramps, sweats, nervousness and headache were back. Jack smiled at me and said, "Duke will make you feel fine again little guy as soon as we get to the apartment and he gives you another shot.

As I entered the apartment Duke was awaiting. He could see I was dripping with perspiration and bent over with cramps. He immediately led me into his bedroom, took my shoes and socks off and began to feel between my toes as he looked up at me and said,

"Damn Joey Boy, you are indeed a mess today alright! I have just the thing here to make you feel all well and perky again babe." He continued to press his fingers between my toes and said, "Sure enough, you're system is crying out for another shot of Duke's magic potent to get you feeling all chipper again Joey! A couple more shots today should make you mine Joey and get you all happy and feeling great again. What say we get those horrible cramps, sweats, headache and nervousness under control first thing, and then we can have some fun again as we did yesterday with the boys. Good thing you got to me when you did today or you may have lost your lunch too baby!"

"Why are you poking around between my toes for Duke?" He rubbed my back, put my head on his shoulder and continued. "Joey, the shots I gave you yesterday, a powerful drug called heroin is very addictive and you are suffering from what is called, 'The Withdrawals' right now. They can get bad, very bad when your system needs another shot or fix Babe! Now I am going to have to teach you how to give yourself a fix when you need one. You watch exactly what I do and next time I will watch you as you give yourself the shot to make sure you do it right." When I realized what Duke had just told me I leaned over, grabbed my shoes and bolted for the door calling him four letter words! He yelled, "You won't get far Joey hurting like you do - come back now and let Duke give you your fix and make you into his pretty and newest pussy-boy whore employee."

I only made it halfway down the hall headed for the exit door. Jack and Paul grabbed me, dragged me kicking and shouting back into the bedroom and sat me down on the bed next to Duke. Paul chuckled and said, "Look who is back for his 'happy shot' boss!" Jack got behind me, held my arms down to my sides with his arms around my waist. Paul knelt on his knees in front of me, lifted my one foot up on my knee and held it there as he clamped his thighs around my other leg so I was pinned in place. Duke returned from the dresser with the syringe in his one hand and the rubber tubing in the other. "Now you watch real close Joey Boy so you learn how to do this! We do it between the toes so you don't have little ugly needle marks or black and blue spots on you arms or body. That is bad in this business!

Would you want a guy with needle marks all over him fucking with you? I don't think so!" He made sure I was watching as he put the rubber around my ankle and tightened it up. "This is to stop the blood flow and make the vein bulge so I can find a good red one crying out for a poke with this here syringe full of the magic potion that already has made you my obedient sex slave. Now you make sure the plunger on the syringe is all the way to the bottom so there is no air in the syringe. Otherwise it could put a bubble in your bloodstream and be instant death when the bubble reached your heart. Very important - all the way down! You stick the needle in this little bottle of medicine and pull liquid up into the tube until it gets right to this little red mark I put here for you so you don't get too much. That could kill you too - understand! Then you push the plunger until the air bubbles out of the needle part and any bubbles stop with a clear little flow of fluid. You see this nice big juicy red vein here between these two toes. Just watch how I push the needle quickly but gently into that vein sideways so it does not go all the way through the vein. It must line up inside the vein or you will get a great big ugly black and blue mark where the medicine enters skin tissue. Now you squeeze the little plunger and the medicine makes you feel wonderful again baby. Just like that – a quick and simple fix for all your' troubles darling. You have any questions now?"

I said, "Yea, let me up so I can get out of here for good! I'm not your sex slave and certainly not a druggie for you to control and turn into a full time street hooker."

He smiled and said, "Oh Joey baby, I have big plans for your future Babe. I have another busy day planned for you! No more resistance out of you now!" He backslapped my face and said, "You should be feeling real good again about now baby as the drug kicks in, and I will be increasing your dose a little at a time so you can go for longer periods of time without needing your fix to keep your habit satisfied and the horrible side affects of withdrawal making you feel like did earlier again. We will give you another full day of pleasures beyond you imagination Joey and by the end of today you will be and do anything I ask of you just to get your next fix when needed. Get the clothing off him boys, looks as though our pretty little, cunt boy Joey is going to enjoy another day of pleasures and indoctrination before he succumbs to his new station in life." He looked down into my eyes and said, "After today you will be a heroin junkie Joey Boy and my little slave boy to fuck regularly with the boys when ever we want, but most importantly, I plan to teach you to hustle that hot sexy ass of yours and make us all wealthy. I control the drugs Joey. A couple more shots today and you will crawl if you have to be here every day begging for your shot! You will soon learn to do exactly what I tell you to do. When you need a shot Joey and start hurting, you will know who owns you baby."

Jack and Paul peeled my clothing off and I spent another four hours servicing both of them as Duke continued with the same routine as yesterday. When he had me broken he took me and made love to me again as before, constantly reminding me of his ownership and total control. He obviously kept my dosages small so I had to keep coming back to him each day for another shot for the next week. Each time he watched me to make sure I did it right, then rewarded me by making love to me and telling me how much I meant to him. After a week of servicing him, Jack and Paul on a daily basis he took me back on the corner and taught me how to approach, negotiate and deliver the goods.

I would sneak out every night and run to Duke, leaving excuse after excuse to Master Jake why I could not be in for further training. He finally gave up on me, but Trooper Jerry Gallagher obviously put a trail on me and realized what I was doing. Before I knew it, one night as we were all standing on the corner of California and Polk, the police showed up and ushered us all into a paddy wagon. Trooper Jerry was present and acted like he didn't even know me, but he must have pulled some strings, as the next thing I knew I was in a rehabilitation center going through the torments of withdrawal. He and Grandma Schmidt visited me regularly for the weeks I was in rehab. Grandma never did notified mom or dad of my transgression, but when released, she informed me that Trooper Gallagher saved my butt and probably my life as well. She said he also agreed to take me under his guiding hand to keep my nose clean after my release. She said in return for his help with me, Trooper Jerry would be taking his meals with us each day when he was not working. She further stated I would be living with him in his apartment where he could keep an eye on me when I was not at college. He put a locator band on my ankle and monitored my activities until he felt I could be trusted. A year later he finally removed the belt and we have been living together ever since. When I graduated from S.F. State, he and Grandma Schmidt were so proud of my turnaround. I am now going to law school in the city, getting all the love I need from my one and only Trooper Jerry Gallagher every night, the kind of love we both like. I love the big guy and he loves me too. He continued his dominant ways with me and I just loved him talking dirty to me and treating me roughly when we had sex. That should give you an idea of our relationship when we were alone together in the playroom.

Grandma is a real cool lady. When I finally got around to telling her that I loved Trooper Gallagher she just shrugged her shoulders and said, "I knew that Joey - I not stupid you know!" She put her arms around me and hugged me and added, "I love you Joey, I just want you be alive and happy. You can tell your papa you want, he understand all about such love between men and boys, but don't tell-a-your mama Joey - she no understand, maybe someday she do, but I doubt it very much!"

ABOUT THE AUTHOR

The author was born and raised in a small community in the Sierra Foothills of Northern California where he attended elementary and high school. After completing college and a hitch in the US Army as a draftee, he worked as an accountant for a number of years. He found pushing numbers and restricted to an office environment day after day far too boring and changed careers, working as an executive officer until his retirement in 2001.

Since retirement he has moved back to the community where he was raised to enjoy what some refer to as their golden years. He travels often, works in the garden, attends a cardio therapy exercise class three days a week, and spends a great deal of his time reading, writing and pounding the piano ivories.

"Virgin Army Boy Deflowered" was his first published book, after having a few short stories posted on a free web site on the Internet over a period of years since his retirement. This story, "Cub Boy Training," is his second published alternative lifestyle novel.

Yerlac

Virgin Army Boy Deflowered

VIRGIN ARMY BOY
Deflowered

a novel by
BRET YERLAC

A BONER BOOK

www.ingramcontent.com/pod-product-compliance
Lightning Source LLC
Chambersburg PA
CBHW051126260626
47170CB00005B/1688